First Encounter

It came at Seeker like a blur in the dusk. The pain as it bit into the Novice's leg was shocking and knocked Seeker down to his knees. The blackness came too swiftly to even identify the attacker...

The lizard took a small bite from the leg and chewed happily. Food for several days. It ate carefully, avoiding large veins and arteries or other things that might kill its prey too soon. The lizard wanted to keep his prey alive and fresh as long as possible...

Ace Books by Dennis Schmidt

The Kensho Series

WAY-FARER
KENSHO
SATORI
WANDERER

Twilight of the Gods

TWILIGHT OF THE GODS: THE FIRST NAME
TWILIGHT OF THE GODS II: GROA'S OTHER EYE
TWILIGHT OF THE GODS III: THREE TRUMPS SOUNDING

The Questioner Trilogy

LABYRINTH
CITY OF CRYSTAL SHADOW

**BOOK TWO OF
THE QUESTIONER TRILOGY**

CITY OF CRYSTAL SHADOW

DENNIS SCHMIDT

ACE BOOKS, NEW YORK

This book is an Ace original edition,
and has never been previously published.

CITY OF CRYSTAL SHADOW

An Ace Book/published by arrangement with
the author

PRINTING HISTORY
Ace edition/April 1990

All rights reserved.
Copyright © 1990 by Dennis Schmidt.
Cover art by Rowena Morril.
This book may not be reproduced in whole or in part,
by mimeograph or any other means, without permission.
For information address: The Berkley Publishing Group,
200 Madison Avenue, New York, New York 10016.

ISBN: 0-441-69779-8

Ace Books are published by the Berkley Publishing Group,
200 Madison Avenue, New York, New York 10016.
The name "ACE" and "A" logo are trademarks
belonging to Charter Communications, Inc.

PRINTED IN THE UNITED STATES OF AMERICA

10 9 8 7 6 5 4 3 2 1

*This book is dedicated to Miriam
and to Uncle George.
They didn't have to help, but they did.*

Every questioning is a seeking.
Every seeking takes its direction beforehand
from what is sought.

> Martin Heidegger,
> *Being and Time*

CITY OF CRYSTAL SHADOW

Prologue

*The world is deep,
Deeper than day had been aware.
Deep is its woe;
Joy—deeper yet than agony:
Woe implores: Go!
But all joy wants eternity—
Wants deep, wants deep eternity.*

        Friedrich Nietzsche,
        Thus Spoke Zarathustra

※⊱❀⊰※

Longarm's thick lips puckered out in a hoot of laughter. It danced two quick shuffle steps on its short, bandy legs and, its arms waving about with high good humor, slapped the ground twice with long-fingered hands. "Expected something big and grand, eh?" the Teacher chortled.

Seeker shook its head. "Well, not big and grand exactly."

"But not tiny and shabby," Bilrog growled. "Are you sure that damned thing will survive Jump? Looks like a piece of junk left over from the First Empire."

The Teacher nodded enthusiastically. "Exactly. It looks like a piece of floating junk. Nothing worth bothering with. Trash. Whole thing is totally shielded against leaking any kind of radiation. Nothing comes out. No ultralong waves, no ultrahigh frequencies, nothing. The ship can't send any kind of message. There's nothing on board but a receiver that can be tuned to the Call frequencies. The whole ship appears as dead as a chunk of interstellar flotsam. Cold, lifeless piece of rock. It could float through any system without causing the least comment. And without having a bunch of patrol ships blast it.

"Look, you two. Did it ever occur to either of you that Labyrinth is the easy part of being a Questioner? You come here as a Pretender and try to go from Start to Sanctuary. All that happens is that the planet tries to kill you. No big problem. You either make it or you die. If you die, no big problem. If you make it, ah, then you become a Novice and you have a big problem." Longarm chuckled and grinned. "Oh, yes, a big, big problem!"

Bilrog scowled, an expression that seemed natural on the creature's harsh face. Heavy brows lowered above small keen eyes that lay on either side of a long snout. The grim slash of a mouth, filled with sharp, pointed teeth, was pulled downward at its corners. The head itself was large and rounded, rising from heavy shoulders on a thick neck. Dark, short fur covered the face and the rest of the barrellike body, which rested on two round, powerful legs. The arms were strongly muscled and ended in hands of six fingers, each tipped with retractable claws. "Labyrinth was a pretty big problem as far as I'm concerned. It was a final problem for Thisunit and Darkhider. And for H*mb*l, too, in a way."

Seeker shuddered. "Nearly got me. Yes, Bilrog is right. Labryinth killed Thisunit and Darkhider. And... and it did something to H*mb*l as well. Something strange. H*mb*l might as well be dead! The hummer hasn't got a chance in the long run. It's... it's just out there, dancing. I..." Seeker stopped in confusion, surprised at the strength of its own emotions.

Longarm made an impatient gesture, but the Teacher's tone was mild and kind. "Huh! Still worried about the hummer, eh? Best worry about yourself more and less about the dancer. H*mb*l can take care of itself. Huh! You should do half so well." Longarm sighed deeply. "Ah, but good advice never did penetrate your thick skull, Seeker. You'll worry about H*mb*l until you figure it all out, won't you?"

Seeker nodded slowly. "I can accept what happened to Thisunit and Darkhider. They tried and failed. But H*mb*l was the best of us all. The hummer didn't fail. Couldn't. And yet ... there it is dancing out there, facing death every instant. Why doesn't it come back in? It knows the way to Sanctuary. Labyrinth must be holding it somehow. I just don't understand."

"H*mb*l was your friend," Longarm said softly. "The hummer has made a choice. You don't have to understand, Seeker. You just have to accept."

Seeker shook its head. "Accept? I can't do that, Teacher.

City of Crystal Shadow 5

Labyrinth took Darkhider and Thisunit. It almost got Bilrog and me. It still holds H*mb*l.'' Seeker paused thoughtfully. "And perhaps it still holds us as well. Perhaps it never lets go completely." Seeker paused again, then continued. "But in any case, Teacher, Labyrinth could hardly be called the easy part of anything. It could only be easy if there was something worse, and what could be worse?"

Longarm laughed derisively. "Oh, there's worse, all right. Worse and worse and worse and worse . . . right out to the ends of the universe. It's called Life, and it's the worst problem of them all. And right out into the middle of it is where you're going. If you think Labyrinth was deadly . . . Hah!

"You're Novices now. That means you get into one of those"—the Teacher gestured to the decrepit-looking ship— "sail off into space, Jump to a randomly chosen system, listen for a Call. If there is one, you go to the planet making the Call, park your ship in a nice obscure orbit, get into the transfer unit, and zip! your mind is sent down into the host. Then you try to solve the problem that made for the Call."

"Doesn't sound any worse than Labyrinth to me," Bilrog rumbled. "Huh. Sounds like a vacation in comparison."

Longarm whooped with hilarity, sputtering and choking, waving its long arms around, pounding the dusty ground with its flat feet. "Vacation? Vacation? Ah, ah, Bilrog, you are without a doubt the stupidest Novice I've ever met! It's nothing less than a wonder you made it twenty feet out of Start! A vacation? Ah, yes, a vacation indeed!"

Seeker looked confused. "But nothing you said seemed to be a problem. It . . ."

"I take it back. Bilrog isn't the stupidest. You are! No problems, eh? Think, you fools! The ship Jumps at random. What if it puts you into a hostile system? Eh? And patrol vessels shoot you out of space? Eh? What if you get a signal and it's just a decoy? What if what they want to do is kill a Questioner? Eh? There are creatures like that in the universe, you know. Kill anything, just for the fun of it. What if the signal is an old one and the problem is so far gone you can't solve it and they kill your host? You die, too, you know. What if your host is unstable and goes crazy during the sharing? You'll probably end up trapped and insane yourself!

"Oh, it's endless. Endless. There are lots of ways to die here on Labyrinth. A whole planetful of ways. But out there, out in the universe, there are a lot more ways. And some of them are so strange you won't even know what they are until you're already dying. Why in the name of the Primordial Tree do you think the kill rate is so high for Novices?"

Bilrog returned Seeker's glance. The Furmorian warrior lifted heavy eyebrows and rolled its eyes skyward. "Either our Teacher is trying to scare caution into us, or else it is worried about our health."

Seeker bared its teeth in a grin. "Sounds mighty like a Nurturer to me. Fretting over cubs."

"Ahhhhh, you're hopeless, the both of you!" Longarm groaned, a huge grin splitting its face. "The worst crop of Novices I've ever seen! But then, you're all I have to work with, so you'll have to do."

"What were you like as a Novice?" Seeker asked innocently.

The Teacher stared at the ursoid. "Me? Why, I was . . . That is, I . . . Oh, by the Tree, I was worse than either of you! Hah! And that's the truth!"

The three of them exploded into laughter. "Ah, ah, what a rogue and fool I was!" Longarm gasped out. "Thought I'd take on the universe and solve every problem in about a week." The simian creature stopped laughing as memory came flooding into its mind. "Ah, yes, and then I went out." Longarm shuddered. "My first contact, my first mission."

"You made it," Bilrog chuckled.

Longarm turned on him, eyes flashing, brow furrowed darkly. "Oh, yes, I made it. Mostly I did. I failed, you see, miserably. The whole planet went up. I barely escaped. But they all died. All of them. Because I failed. I spent a good year back here recovering. I was a mess, mentally, physically, spiritually. A mess. They almost didn't let me go out a second time. But I went eventually. Ah, yes, I went."

"And you succeeded?" Seeker asked softly.

"Huh. Succeeded? I survived, and that's saying a lot. But succeeded? I'm not too sure I know what that means anymore. I asked questions, offered a solution, they sent me away."

"Did they . . . did they accept it?" Bilrog asked.

Longarm shrugged. "Don't know. They sent me back to the ship and I Jumped out of there as soon as I could get power up." The Teacher sighed. "Look, Bilrog, creatures don't always want a solution to their problems. Especially not one that's painful. And they aren't always grateful when you give them one, Questioner or not."

"They weren't grateful?" Seeker questioned.

Longarm scowled. "I was helped through Jump by a burst of energy. Gave me kind of an extra shove."

Bilrog hissed a curse. "They shot at you?"

The Teacher nodded. "I told you I Jumped as soon as I could. If I'd been a little slower the missile would have blown me apart rather than pushing me on to my next assignment. That one went better, at least."

The two Novices were silent. "Huh." Longarm blew a puff of air between its thick lips. "So. Now you begin to see. But you won't really understand until you're well into your first mission. We're dealing with life here. And that means we're dealing with death just as surely. Ours, theirs, everyone's."

"Sentience," Seeker whispered.

"Sentience?" the Teacher hooted. "Sentience? Sentience has nothing much to do with it. Sentience just tells you something about the habits of a species. It doesn't make them good or bad, friendly or hostile, sane or crazy. All the species you'll deal with will have sentience of some sort. But most of them will be species whose sentience has backed them into a corner, a corner they can't get out of on their own. That's why they've sent out the Call. Oh, yes, they're sentient. And they're scared and angry and desperate. Hah. Any trapped animal is dangerous. A sentient trapped animal is ten times as dangerous.

"But enough of this light chatter. I don't want to make you think being a Novice is all fun and games. Let's go aboard the ship and do some real work. Like learning how to set the Jump, power on and off, prepare the stasis tank, calibrate the transfer unit, work the life support systems. All those little things your existence depends on once you get into your Jumpship and take off for parts unknown."

"Uh, when do we leave?" Bilrog asked.

"As soon as I can get you out of here," Longarm snapped. "There are an infinite number of problems out there waiting for a Questioner to at least try to solve. Here you're doing nobody any good. Out there you can at least be dying."

In the City

*Truth is the kind of error
without which a certain species of life
  could not live.
The value for life is ultimately decisive.*

> Friedrich Nietzsche,
> The Will to Power

I.

The stasis unit woke the sole occupant of the Jumpship as it reentered realspace out toward the edges of the system. There the magnetic and gravitational tides which swept around stars with planets were relatively calm and the dangers of re-entry greatly lessened. Going into Jump was possible from almost anywhere, provided there were no massive gravity wells close at hand. Ships that tried to Jump from near a star tended to end up inside the star or were randomly pitched to some utterly unknown and uncharted destination from which few had ever returned. But re-entry was a different matter. Popping into existence as a mass in realspace was always safest when one was as far as possible from other masses. The edges of systems were thus generally the re-entry points. Actually, no one was too sure whether it was mass or gravity or magnetic fields which caused the problems, but since they were all just different ways of looking at the same thing, it didn't really make any difference.

As the occupant slowly awoke, the Jumpship put out its sensitive ears and eyes and began to collect data. It listened especially carefully for a particular signal on a narrow band of frequencies used for only one purpose. Every bit of information was examined, correlated, and then evaluated and stored for the moment when the occupant would be ready to examine them.

The creature that finally emerged from the stasis tank was a honey-colored ursoid, almost six feet tall and nearly as wide. Despite its bulk, it moved with a fluid grace that indicated great power well under control. Two large soft brown eyes brimming with the light of intelligence were on either side of a short snout tipped with a black nose. The mouth was filled with sharp, dangerous-looking teeth. Long muscular arms ended in hands with strong stubby fingers. The legs were short and stout, giving it a solid, firm stance. Low on the front of the furry body were six bulges in two rows of three each. As it gazed around the cabin of the Jumpship, a bright red comb quickly rose on the top of its head, then subsided.

"Good welcome, Novice," the Jumpship's computer intoned. "We trust you rested well?"

"Well enough," the Novice rumbled. "One can't expect totally sweet dreams when in Jump."

"True," the ship replied, "but the experience is much worse when conscious. Few species can survive such a twisting of the mind. Only arachnids seem capable of it on a regular basis."

"Useful information," the Novice replied drily, realizing even as it spoke that its sarcasm was wasted on the computer.

"Would you care for further data on this subject?"

"Uh, no. Just a review of this system, if you don't mind."

"Very well, Novice. Catalogue Reference AZT56801DPP. Five planets around a blue star, type XX34b. First planet, barren, average temperature 785 Universal, no atmosphere. Second planet, barren, average temperature 276 Universal, no atmosphere. Third planet, arid, average temperature 145 Universal, atmosphere, oxygen, nitrogen, carbon oxide mon and di, traces of methane, argon, helium, hydrogen. Fourth planet, gas giant. Fifth planet, barren, average temperature 31 Universal, no atmosphere. System discovered by probe, date 20789 Universal. No sentients indicated. No further contact since the probe mission."

"Hmmm. Not too promising. Worse than the last two systems, and they were empty. Any life sign?"

"Life potential on Three. Investigation requested?"

The Novice sighed. "Of course. Let's go to Call range and check it out. Probably another deader. Huh. The Teacher told us this would be difficult. But it never mentioned that it would be so damn boring! Five systems so far. Two deaders. One hostile. One primitive. And now this one." The ursoid stretched and yawned, its teeth glittering in the harsh light of the small cabin. "Wonder how many I'll have to hit before I get a..."

"Call, Novice," the computer interrupted. "From the third planet."

The Novice froze in its stretch. "Call?" it responded, its voice soft with wonder. "A real Call?"

"Yes, on Band 12. Date of sending commencing... local time, eight turns ago."

"Turns? Of the planet?"

"Of the system."

"Ah, years, then. Eight years. Not too long."

"Scanning planet. Major power source, and signal source, single location, northeast quadrant."

"How about some more on the planet? Show the data on the screens while you summarize."

"Arid, no open bodies of water, not much atmospheric moisture. Surface mainly silicon-based rock, little metal." The ursoid watched the numbers flash up on the screen that filled the far end of the cabin. "Gravity .7668 your norm. Atmosphere too thin your norm. Oxygen only 32%. Diameter 7,556 miles. No satellites, but a thin ring of rocky detritus, some ice. Tilt, .004 degrees. Estimate marginally habitable."

"Nice place," the ursoid muttered. "Cold, dry, and desolate. Yet there's a Call, eh? A real Call?"

"Affirmative. Shall we approach?"

"That's what we're here for!" An edge of excitement crept into the Novice's voice. "Yes, by Labyrinth! That's what we're here for! Set up orbit within the ring. Seems like a safe place."

"Ring orbit would be optimal for secrecy. We would be one of the larger chunks, but not noticeably so. Approach will take two weeks, Universal, two and a half, local."

"Good, good. Time to ready the transfer unit. I wonder what kind of creatures they are? And what their problem is? What does the Call say?"

"The Call is on Band 12, Novice. Band 12 carries no message. It's just a call for help, without priority rating."

"Ummm, yes, Band 12. Remember it now. So it's not a plague or medical emergency. Not war either. Hmmm. Could be almost anything else, though. Anything that wouldn't require a priority rating. Well, let's go. Slowly, slowly, so as not to attract attention. Two weeks, eh? Hmmm. Plenty of time.''

From the ring, the northern hemisphere of the planet filled the view from the Jumpship's single porthole. It was dull beige in color, cloudless, waterless, seemingly lifeless. Yet the Novice knew that was not the case. There was life down there. Especially in the northeast quadrant.

The ursoid called up the screen again and gazed in wonder at the magnified picture displayed there. A vast city, soaring skyward in incredible towers; leaping bridges; slender, yearning spires; faceted, glittering surfaces, stretching up and up there in the midst of the desert. A city of crystal that shone and glittered in the relentless sunlight. A giant, multihued jewel of almost unimaginable beauty in the midst of endless beige desolation. The city was the source of the Call, the origin of the cry for help that had spread out and out into the cold emptiness of space for eight years. The Call that was now answered.

The Novice switched off the screen with a sigh and a slight shudder. It was time to go down to the surface of the planet, and suddenly the ursoid felt uncertain. Who or what am I to go down there and offer my help? Just because I managed to survive Labyrinth doesn't mean I can solve their problem, doesn't even mean I can understand it! And what does it mean to survive Labyrinth anyway? It was just a fluke in my case, a mistake. H*mb*l was the one that should have made it, not me! And yet H*mb*l dances still, swaying and swirling slowly across the face of death.... And I sit here in a scout ship and stare at the face of an alien planet that has sent out a cry for help. What help can I offer, what hope? How can I answer their questions when I can't even answer my own?

Yet I'm going. The creature gazed at the chamber attached to the transfer unit. Its body would lie in there while its mind was down on the planet sharing the mind of whatever host had been prepared for it. Whenever a signal was sent out, a host was prepared in anticipation of the arrival of help.

The ursoid shook its head in wonder. I will be in the mind and body of another creature. What will it be like? There was no way of knowing, no way of even anticipating. The Teacher had hinted that there could be dreadful problems involved.

City of Crystal Shadow

Transfer into a mind that was too alien could lead to insanity for both host and guest. But Band 12 wasn't one of the exotic bands. Not like 3 or 7 or 1, the bands specially reserved for sapient arachnids. Yet still . . . there were problems. *And what will my mind be like afterward? Will I still be the same? Or will I be subtly changed, slightly, just ever so slightly different, just ever so slightly like* it?

A shudder lightly shook the huge body. *Ah, H*mb*l, H*mb*l, it should be you that is here. You, so you could dance their questions and through the fluid grace of your dips and sways and twirls provide the answers they need. But you dance far, far away. Why? Why?*

It looked once more at the beige surface of the planet. *What is waiting down there for me? Success? Failure? Life? Death? Joy? Horror?* It sighed deeply yet again. *The longer I wait, the worse the anticipation becomes. There's really no excuse for continuing to delay. H*mb*l would not have hesitated.* It cleared its throat and spoke to the ship. "Ready for transfer."

"Ready, Novice," came the impersonal reply. "Enter the chamber and make the necessary attachments."

"Huh," the ursoid replied, muttering beneath its breath. "Easy for you to say." Then, louder, it asked, "What will you do while I'm gone?"

"Maintain the ship. And sustain the life of the organism in the chamber until transfer is terminated."

"Terminated?"

"Affirmative. Until the Novice returns to the ship. Or fails to return and the mission is aborted."

"Aborted?"

"Affirmative. If the Novice ceases to exist on the face of the planet, the mission is aborted, the corpse in the chamber is ejected and the ship returns to base."

"Ah, ejected, yes," the ursoid grunted noncommittally as it moved slowly toward the chamber. "Uh, but how will you know when to bring me back? I mean, how will you know if the mission succeeds?"

"The Novice's thought patterns will be constantly monitored while on the surface of the planet. When the Novice is aware that the mission is completed, it will be recalled."

"But how do you know I won't cheat if the going gets rough and pretend the mission is complete?"

"Novices do not behave in that manner."

"Why not, when their lives are threatened?" the ursoid asked, a slight edge of exasperation creeping into its voice. "How do you know Novices won't behave in that manner?"

"The fact that you will not was well established by your performance on Labyrinth. Had you been the type to run from danger, you never would have reached Sanctuary. Novices do not behave in such a fashion. Besides," it continued after a slight pause, "there are safeguards built into the monitoring system."

"Hmmm," the Novice mused as it crawled into the chamber. "So you trust us. But only so far, eh?" The computer was silent.

"Good luck, Novice," the computer said just before the lid of the chamber closed on the recumbent figure. "That is, if your species has such a concept."

Eyelids fluttered. Eyes opened. Three of them. The light was bright and liquid in texture, shot through with crystalline tones. Looking upward. Toward the sky. Empty sky.

A face came into view. Known. Narrow, two big reddish eyes on either side of the beak, the third, pale blue, higher in the forehead. Grey feathers covering the crown and flaring out at the sides. Beak blue with streaks of yellow, slightly hooked and canted to the left. Thryimm.

"Are you there, Questioner?" The voice was high and clear, made for calling on the wind. "Have you arrived safely?"

"I . . . yes . . . disoriented a bit."

"Ah, yes, yes. Good, good. I am Thryimm. Your host is Thassyil. It is suppressed right now to allow you time to find your way around the mind and body."

"Kind . . . very kind . . . thank you. Where . . . where are we?"

"We are at the top of Dhillmyir Eyrie in the Nest of Thyillmyir of the Brood Soorthyir in the Crystal City of the Vyinnlyirr, the People of Light and Air. And have you an individual designation?"

"Desig . . . oh, a name? Yes. I am called Seeker."

"And you have come in answer to our Call, Seeker?"

"Yes."

Thryimm trilled delightedly. "The Leader will be so pleased to hear it. It has been eight years since we set the beacon. We were beginning to wonder if a Questioner would ever arrive."

Seeker sat up slowly and gazed down at the body it inhabited. It was long, at least seven feet tall, and very thin. Narrow arms extended from the shoulders. Three fourths of the way out on the arm, four fingers spread out, lightly clawed and multijointed. A fifth finger extended beyond for perhaps six more inches. Attached to it, and to the whole lower edge of the arm, was a thin membrane that reached back to the body, running from beneath the shoulder to the hip. The hips were narrow. Beneath them were skinny legs, covered with scales, that ended in clawlike feet with seven toes. Except for the legs, the whole body was covered with a soft, downlike substance, grey and mottled brown in color.

Thryimm stood watching, its head cocked to one side as if listening to its own shoulder. Occasionally it nodded as if pleased. "So," it finally said, "do you approve of your host? It is a fine specimen of the Vyinnlyirr, the People of Light and Air. Yes, Thassyil is one of our best."

"Gender?" Seeker asked.

"Gender?" Thryimm paused thoughtfully. "Hmmm. Ah, yes, I understand. An ancient word, undoubtedly dragged up by you from the depths of Thassyil's racial memory. No longer applies, you see. We no longer have gender or sexes. We developed beyond that stage many eons ago. It made no sense, was illogical, messy, and uncertain. The Leader can explain all that to you later. But, no, Thassyil has no gender. There are no gender taboos to worry about, Questioner. How thoughtful of you to ask, though."

Seeker moved its limbs slowly, getting used to their feel. It glanced questioningly at the membrane. "And this?"

"Ah, yes, yes. Once we flew. And then glided. But now our wings are simply ornamental, things of beauty. Don't you find them so? Thassyil has an especially fine set."

Seeker looked at them. They did indeed seem fine. Seeker lifted its arms and watched the membrane, thin and semitransparent, spread out. It caught the light and glistened with many colors. "Ah, yes, very fine." Carefully, gently, Seeker slipped over the edge of the table and stood. "Huh, I can stand without any trouble." It took two slow steps forward, two back. "And walk, too. So far, so good. When will Thassyil's mind be free again?"

Thryimm looked up at the light in the sky. "In two discwidths it will begin to return, slowly, groggily. It might be a bit disoriented and frightened at first. For that reason, it might be best to visit with the Leader right away so that you will have time to be alone with Thassyil when it comes back. An adjustment and accommodation time, so to speak. Time to become firm nestmates, for truly, more than any others ever, you two share the same nest."

Seeker nodded agreement. "Yes, I would like to go and meet the Leader now. You have been waiting eight years for your Call to be answered. I'm here now and would like to begin."

"Begin? Ah, well, yes, but there is no hurry as to that. First you must meet the Leader, yes. Perhaps that is the best place to begin, if beginning it is. Yes, but no hurry. No. No hurry." Thryimm turned and gestured for Seeker to follow. "This way, if you please. I'm sure the Leader is waiting."

They left the Eyrie through an arched opening in one wall. "No door?" Seeker asked politely.

"Door?" Thryimm responded, puzzled. "The word has no real meaning for us. Do you mean a way to shut a nest off from the rest of the city? Ah, yes, you do. But that is not necessary among us, you see. We do not have private things in that sense. Nests are for all, not just for one. There are more than enough nests here in the city, so conflicts over occupancy never arise. No, we have no need for doors. Everything is open to everyone."

They stepped out onto an open walkway. The walkway led to a thin bridge that soared dizzyingly across empty space. Like the rest of the city, the bridge was of seemingly fragile crystal, and the light of the sun which now shone almost directly overhead transformed it into a veil of coruscating colors. Everywhere Seeker gazed, light—soft, brilliant, multi-hued, shimmering light, bent into rainbows by the crystal, shattered into a billion fragments by the faceted surfaces—filled the air and the eye and almost seemed to fill the mind and body as well. The effect was staggering.

Seeker stopped on the bridge, gripping the rail to steady itself, suddenly overwhelmed by it all. Thryimm turned back with a short trill of concern. "Is all in order, Questioner? Are you feeling quite well? Did we leave the nest too swiftly? Would you like to return?"

"I . . . it is all so beautiful . . . I've never seen anything like it. Never even dreamed of anything like it." Seeker looked down over the low wall of the bridge. The depths beneath it were aswirl with brilliance and hue. "The light breaks... in a billion colors. Flows, recombines, leaps from point to point. It... it seems a thing alive."

Thryimm's trill was smug and satisfied. "Yes, yes. So nice of you to notice. The city is light and air, you see, for we are the Children of Light and Air. The city is our greatest accomplishment, our ultimate triumph. It embodies the spirit, the soul, the very meaning of the Vyinnlyirr. Yes. It is beautiful. You are very privileged to be able to see it through Thassyil's eyes, through our own eyes, as it were. I mean no offense, but I doubt the eyes of your own species are as sensitive to light as ours. We see far, far into the ultraviolet and deep, deep into the infrared. The colors and hues you are enjoying through our eyes cannot even be sensed by most species. No, indeed. Yes, yes, you are indeed privileged." With that Thryimm trilled again and turned, stalking slowly, smoothly over the bridge.

For what seemed a long time, they crossed sweeping bridges, entered glittering towers, ascended, descended, turned and twisted their way across the Crystal City. Seeker never tired of the view and every step seemed to reveal a new and more astonishing beauty. Truly, the ursoid thought, remembering the ruin of its own planet, these Vyinnlyirr, these Children of Light and Air are a superior species. To even build a city like this implied a technology far advanced over anything Seeker had ever seen or heard of. If, as Thryimm says, this city represents their souls, they must be close to gods. How can a race like this need help from a Questioner? What can a Questioner possibly offer them? And yet, despite all this beauty, despite the obvious technological superiority, there was something... something that Seeker couldn't quite place... something odd and wrong about the city... something.... Then they would come to a new vista, the light and color would surge and overwhelm with its beauty, and all doubt was driven from Seeker's dazzled mind.

Seeker finally realized that their trip was taking them lower and lower into the city, down toward the base of the soaring towers. Yet even further from the sun, the light swooped and swirled, ricocheting from the shining surfaces and shattering into endless brilliance.

They arrived at an opening and Thryimm gave a short, whistling trill. A short, piping cry answered and they entered a hall filled with ruby red air that pulsed and whirled. At the far end stood another of the creatures, taller, grander, and older, much older, than Thryimm. Seeker's guide stopped, raised its membranes so the red light glimmered and shone from them. The creature on the other end of the hall responded with a similar gesture. "Leader," Thryimm trilled in a high pitched voice that slipped easily through the ruby light, "I bring the Questioner."

"We thank you, Thryimm. A blessing on your nest." Thryimm raised its membranes again, then turned and left without a word or a glance at Seeker.

For several moments total silence reigned in the hall. Seeker stood stock still, unsure of what to do or say. Then the Leader clucked its tongue lightly and spoke. "Come, come, approach. I shan't peck you! Ah, ah, Thassyil always was a shy one, and it seems some of it carries over even to a visitor in Thassyil's mind."

Feeling rather foolish, Seeker moved forward across the hall to where the Leader stood waiting. "Yes, yes, yes," the Leader murmured softly as Seeker approached, "you move very like one of us, but not quite. No. One could never see you flying. You are a creature of the earth."

"I very nearly flew once," Seeker said quietly. "I was fleet as the wind, the fastest Chaser on the plain and I almost flew. Not like a glidewing, of course, but..."

"Yes, yes!" the Leader cried out with pleasure. "Yes, now you are moving more like one who could fly indeed! Glidewing, eh? Once we flew, when we were smaller. Then when we grew, we glided. Now only our minds and spirits soar. But, oh, how they soar!"

"I have seen your city. Your spirits do indeed soar."

"Thank you, Questioner, you are indeed kind to say so. Is your host satisfactory? Ah, good, good. And our city? How do you like our city?"

"Magnificent. I lack words to praise it enough."

"Ah, there are no words, no, not even in our language, a language attuned to light and air, to describe the city adequately. It can only be experienced."

"Thryimm told me it was your race's greatest accomplishment, your spirit and your soul. What did it mean by that?"

The Leader paused. "Yes, yes, Thryimm was right. It is indeed that, though since Thryimm is a limited creature, its vision is equally limited.

"The city, you see, is our greatest accomplishment, the culmination of our race's intelligence and ability. But our soul, the soul of the Vyinnlyirr, well, that lies elsewhere, yes, elsewhere, though Thryimm is not far from right, yes, not far."

Seeker stood and looked curiously at the Leader. How strange, the Novice thought. They send out a Call for a Questioner and then when one arrives they greet it kindly enough, walk it through an empty city and then introduce it not to an emergency committee or something, but to only one creature . . .

An empty city! By my six pouches, Seeker suddenly realized, that's what was bothering me! So far the only two Vyinnlyirr I've seen have been Thryimm and the Leader. And Thassyil, my host, of course. I've passed through many streets, over several arching bridges, past opening after opening and never seen a single inhabitant! Could it be that in this entire city there were only three Vyinnlyirr? "Are you a numerous race?" Seeker asked cautiously.

"Hmmm. Numerous, no. Not numerous. Why do you ask?"

"Well, on the way here I never saw another living creature. Only the light and the color."

"Ah, truly the Questioner is observant. There are but few of us. In all this city there are only a few hundred thousand of us."

Seeker cocked its head to one side and looked quizzically at the Leader. "Only a few hundred thousand in this vast city? Are there more of you in other cities, then?"

"More? Other cities? Oh, no, no. There are no more. And there are no other cities. Only this one."

Only a few hundred thousand on the whole planet, then! Seeker thought. And all in this one city. That meant that the beige wastes were lifeless, even as it had suspected when viewing them from the Jumpship. "The . . . the rest of your world is empty?"

"Empty and desolate," the Leader answered smugly. "Nothing sentient can live there. Oh, there are a few species of poisonous reptiles and insects, nothing worth discussing. The city is everything, you see. The city is everything."

"Then the Call definitely came from here. Does . . . does the number of your people have anything to do with the Call? Does..."

"Call? Oh, yes," the Leader interrupted, "oh, yes, the Call. It came from here, yes. I will have Thryimm take you to see the Sender if you are interested. It is in a beautiful tower, high, high in the city where the light is at its very purest. You do love the pure light, don't you? But of course you do. You're in Thassyil's mind, and Thassyil loved the pure light, so you must also love it."

The Leader turned and touched a place on the wall of crystal. "But you must be tired now and soon Thassyil will be awakening and the two of you must get to know each other." Thryimm appeared, walking up the hall. "Here, Thryimm will guide you to your quarters, ah, to Thassyil's nest, where you will stay while you are with us, yes. I will see you later when you are rested." With that, the Leader strode swiftly away into the glowing light.

"Come," Thryimm said, "I will guide you. Thassyil has a very fine nest. I am sure you will like it immensely."

As Seeker followed Thryimm from the hall, its mind was whirling almost as fast as the light. How strange this all was! The creatures in the city had clearly been the ones to send out the Call. And yet no one seemed the least bit anxious to even discuss the matter! In fact, Seeker realized, they seemed determined to talk of almost anything but the Call. It was strange and unexpected. And Seeker remembered clearly that Longarm had said many times that the unexpected was always the most dangerous.

II.

There was a strange flitting about the edges of Seeker's mind. Thassyil, the Novice thought, must be coming back to consciousness.

Welcome, Seeker said. Welcome back and thank you for being my host. A high, keening wail was the reply. There was a dashing about, a frenzy like that of a bird trying to fly through transparent glass to the light and freedom it can see just on the other side of the unyielding surface it cannot penetrate or understand. The Novice was surprised. Thassyil, it said with gentle concern, be calm. It is only the Questioner, the one you are host to. Be calm. There is no danger.

Danger, wailed a thin, piping voice. Danger, oh horror, crippled wings, falling and falling, burning sun, predators, shattered eggs, nest slipping in the high wind...

Stop it! Seeker demanded, surprised at its own forcefulness. But it also knew it had no choice. Thassyil sounded as if it were going insane... and if the host went insane... Be calm, Seeker ordered. There is nothing to fear.

Nothing? came the meek reply. Who... what are you? Why ... why are you in my mind?

The Novice was surprised again. Why, I'm here because you are my host. You agreed to share with me and I came...

A sudden suspicion struck Seeker. Thassyil, you did know I was coming, didn't you? You did volunteer to be my host?

A thoughtful silence followed. Volunteer? came a question. I . . . there is no word in my mind for this idea. Thryimm and the Leader told me I had to do something, something I couldn't understand, but they said it was very important for the brood, that it had to be done and that I had been chosen because my wings were the most beautiful and the guest must be honored so it would be willing to . . . The train of thought broke off suddenly, worriedly. You . . . are you the guest they spoke of?

Yes, Seeker replied, trying to project warmth. I am the Questioner the Call was put out to bring. Do you know why the Call was sent, Thassyil?

Thassyil's thoughts became hidden and furtive. Call? I know where the Sender is. In a tower where the light is wonderful. You should have Thryimm take us to it. Look, from my balcony I can show it to you . . .

Thassyil, the Novice gently interrupted, do you know why the Call was made?

The Vyinnlyirr groaned slightly. Why do you ask me? Ask Thryimm or the Leader. They would be able to tell you. I am only Thassyil of the Beautiful Wings. I know nothing.

It was a lie, and Seeker knew it. The creature is afraid to tell the truth! I am a Questioner, the Novice said to Thassyil. It is my purpose to ask questions. As my host, you are supposed to help me to both ask and to find answers.

How can I help you? moaned Thassyil plaintively. I know nothing. I am afraid. This pressure of you in my mind is almost more than I can stand! I feel that . . . that . . .

Seeker could sense the rising panic in its host. I am not allowed to interfere with its mind, the Novice reminded itself. That is one of the Prime Directives. I cannot go into it to take what I want from its memory. I cannot force it, control it . . . But what if it is panicking? What if my whole mission is threatened by a damn fool Vyinnlyirr . . . ?

Seeker made a decision. With one swift mental blow, it knocked Thassyil unconscious.

Seeker descended two levels and found itself on a broad avenue suspended in the air and running along in front of several buildings. It began to walk, looking for another Vyinnlyirr. If

Thassyil won't give me any information, perhaps someone else will, it decided.

For several minutes it strode along, the only living being on the avenue. Then it heard a noise behind it, a thin piping whisper as if someone were trying to gain attention but feared being overheard. Seeker turned quickly and saw a hand wave briefly to it from an opening in a wall. Ah, the Novice thought, another Vyinnlyirr. It walked to the opening and gave a call similar to the one Thryimm had given outside the Leader's nest. There was no response. After hesitating for a moment Seeker stepped halfway into the opening and peered inside. There was nothing to be seen.

Suddenly nervous, the Novice stepped back. Could this be a trap? Longarm had emphasized again and again how some races were actually hostile to Questioners. And even if the whole race wasn't hostile, it was perfectly possible that there might be factions on a planet that sent a Call. And that one of those factions might not be above killing a Questioner.

Yet Seeker could feel nothing wrong. The acute senses it had developed while trying to survive on the face of the deadly Labyrinth often warned it of danger that other beings would never even notice. But this was a new environment. Would its senses still work here just as well? Seeker looked around once more. The avenue was empty, not a Vyinnlyirr in sight. I must know more, Seeker told itself. Not knowing is in itself dangerous. I take a chance going into this building in search of information. But I take a chance not going, too. The Novice hesitated. What would H*mb*l have done? it wondered. The hummer would have danced in slowly, seeking out the rhythm, the beat, the melody of the situation. It would have flowed and gently joined the movement around it. I can't do that. But I can move slowly and carefully, trying not to disrupt what rhythms are present. And if I pass on by? Does that make things any different? Or does it disturb things even more? There's no way to know yet. I can only move forward, softly and gently as H*mb*l would have. Seeker stepped through the opening.

The room it entered was bathed in emerald green light with flashes of deep blue. It must be like this deep in the sea, the Novice thought. It looked around and caught sight of a Vyinnlyirr at the other end of the room. The creature was standing poised for flight, its wing membranes tentatively raised in greeting.

Seeker raised its wings in response. "I am Seeker," it said as gently and coaxingly as possible. "Who are you?"

"Syssyir," it responded, "nestmate of Thassyil of the Beautiful Wings. And you must be the guest?"

The Novice nodded and moved across the room in Syssyir's direction. "Indeed I am. Greetings. You know of my coming?"

"Oh, yes, I know of your coming. I helped ready my nestmate for your arrival."

"Ah, then Thassyil knew I was coming as well."

"Knew? Well, not exactly knew. The Leader had ordered Thassyil to prepare the same way the Leader would order one of the Vyinnlyirr to nest. And, of course, Thassyil obeyed. Surely Thassyil has told you all this?"

"Ah, well, not quite that way. Thassyil was a little nervous when it regained consciousness, you see..."

Syssyir gave a short cluck of humor. "Yes, yes, Thassyil would be a bit nervous! Beautiful wings, Thassyil has, but not much else! Not the brightest of the Vyinnlyirr! Oh, I warned the Leader not to use Thassyil. 'Unstable, that one,' I said. 'Not at all the type for a host.' But Thryimm and the Leader knew better. Yes, not surprising. What have you done with Thassyil to calm the fool down?"

"Well, I... put it back to sleep."

Syssyir nodded sagely. "Yes, that's best. It will take Thassyil a while to get used to it. But in the end you'll get on quite well. Thassyil is really a very charming and accommodating Vyinnlyirr, if not terribly smart."

"Obviously you know something about the Call. Can you tell me anything?"

"Tell you? Why, hasn't the Leader explained it to you? But then, of course not! Have you been taken to see the room where the Sender is? The light there is most remarkable..."

"You are the third to tell me that," Seeker interrupted abruptly. "I will go see this wondrous room. But I would like to know why the Call that brought me was made."

Syssyir shrugged its thin shoulders and ruffled its wing membrane. "The city is filled with light and air," it said noncommittally.

"But not with Vyinnlyirr. Are you a dying race? Is that why you sent for a Questioner?"

City of Crystal Shadow

The Vyinnlyirr looked strangely at Seeker. "A dying race? No, we are few, but we are hardly a dying race. Our number is what it is because we carefully control the number of nestings allowed in a lifetime. There are precisely 537,537 of us here in the city. That number was ordained many, many turns ago when the brood first came here."

"Here? To this city?"

Syssyir nodded slowly as if unsure whether or not it had said too much. "Yes. Of course. Where else?"

"Have you always been in this city?"

"All of my life."

"No, I mean your race, not you."

The Vyinnlyirr became silent, shifting nervously from foot to foot. "Perhaps you would like to see the Sender's room now? I will be happy to show you there. I am about to go out and in that direction myself and . . ."

"Why did you call to me?" Seeker demanded in exasperation.

Syssyir blinked in confusion. "Call to you? I didn't call to you. I was here and you walked through the opening and came in. I never called to you."

Seeker opened its mouth to reply, thought better of it and fell silent. "Hmmmm," it finally said. "Well, I won't bother you any more. I think I feel Thassyil coming back again. I will return to its nest and try to deal with my host alone. Good day." Seeker nodded pleasantly to Syssyir, and the creature nodded back. Then the Novice turned and left, its mind racing with surmise.

The sun was no longer overhead. From where Seeker stood, it had slipped more than halfway to the horizon. Dark in another hour or two. The light in the city had already changed subtly, Seeker realized. Redder now, with wonderful overtones of orange and black shooting through it. Would the city turn dark as the sun slid from the sky? Seeker looked around but could see no sign of lights to illuminate the city once the sun was gone. Of course, the Novice thought, I could be looking right at them and not even realize it.

Thassyil had come back to consciousness as Seeker was walking back to the nest. The Vyinnlyirr had been fearful and a bit sheepish, apologizing for its earlier reaction. Seeker had graciously and cautiously accepted, then kept the Vyinnlyirr out of its thoughts and effectively shut off in its own little space.

There is something very strange going on here, Seeker ruminated. I've met four of these creatures so far and although I would wager all four know why the Call was made, not a one of them will tell me the reason. And Syssyir won't even admit to having called out to me. Perhaps I should just go see their damn Sender in its wondrous room and be done with it. Is there some special reason they want me to go there?

As it wandered about the city, Seeker saw a few other Vyinnlyirr, but all of them were in the distance and never ventured close enough to be hailed. They are avoiding me, the Novice decided, staying as far away as possible. But why?

Following Thassyil's directions, it returned to its nest. The sun was almost on the horizon. In a niche in one wall of the nest, Seeker discovered a small pile of pellets which Thassyil informed it were its food for the day. The city sends it, the Vyinnlyirr told the Novice. The city cares for all our needs.

Curious, Seeker asked if the Vyinnlyirr raised any domestic animals or grew any crops for food. Thassyil shuddered with distaste at the idea. No, the creature declared, the city does all that. The Children of Light and Air have been freed from such things ever since the city came into being.

When was that? Seeker asked innocently. Thassyil's mind paused, uncertain. Ask the Leader, came the eventual answer.

Thryimm entered, displayed its wings and spoke. "Shall we go visit the Leader again, Questioner?"

Seeker nodded. "Yes. I think I would like to do that. Thryimm, how long have you lived in this city?"

"All my life."

The Novice sighed. "That's not what I mean. How long have the Vyinnlyirr lived in this city?"

"Ever since it came into being."

"And how long is that?"

"Perhaps twenty thousand years."

Seeker stared at the Vyinnlyirr, speechless at last. "Twenty thousand years?" it said, its voice high and thin with astonishment. "Twenty thousand years in this city?"

"Oh, yes, at least that long," Thryimm said carelessly. "But I know only a little. Ask the Leader if you wish to know more. The Leader or the Keeper of Memories."

City of Crystal Shadow

* * *

The Keeper of Memories was an ancient Vyinnlyirr, its membranes thin and sagging, its downlike covering balding and patchy. "To be exact, 20,459 years. The city was completed 20,459 years ago. But then, it took 10,021 years to build from its first foundation to the final tower. The total age is, hmmmm, 30,470. That would make the Project . . ."

"Ah, the light is wonderful now, Questioner. Come look at it from this window," the Leader called out from across the room. Seeker turned slowly from the Keeper of Memories for a moment to glare at the Leader. When the Novice turned back a moment later, the old Vyinnlyirr was already ten paces away and moving off swiftly without so much as a backward glance.

With a silent curse of frustration, Seeker went over to join the Leader by the window. "You see," the Leader explained as if nothing had happened, "during the absence of our sun, the city produces its own light. Indeed, there are some of us who feel that the city light is actually more beautiful than the sun light. So much more . . . ethereal."

Seeker gazed out of the window and caught its breath. The bright light of the day had been replaced with a softer, more diffuse light that seemed to flow from every wall and surface. Gently it wove a spell of diaphanous beauty through the air. It seemed to glow inwardly, vibrating and pulsing as if alive. It came from nowhere, it came from everywhere. The vibrant colors of the day were muted now, primaries reduced to pastels, softer and more lustrous than any Seeker had ever even imagined. "It . . . it is beautiful," the Novice stammered.

"Yes," the Leader sighed softly. "Yes, so beautiful it makes it all worth it, doesn't it?"

Seeker's mind became alert again. "Makes all what worth it?"

The Leader gestured broadly with one arm. "The waste."

"The waste? Ah, you mean the desert outside the city?"

"Yes. Once, oh, so long ago, that was all living, green, yes, living. Filled with things." The Leader sighed deeply.

"How did it change?" Seeker asked softly, almost afraid to ask for fear the Leader would cease speaking—as it always had when it was asked direct questions.

"Ah, well, we destroyed it, you see. Over a period of ten thousand years we destroyed it."

"Why?"

"To build the city, of course. Yes. We stripped our planet, Questioner, stripped it of everything it contained. Every metal, every mineral, everything. And we put it all into this city. Oh, to build a city like this takes incredible resources. We even gobbled up the satellite that used to circle our world. All that's left is a ring of junk out there. Yes, we used it all. To create the city. To create the greatest beauty the universe has ever known. Look out at it, Questioner. Look and see it. Was it not worth it? Such beauty. Such beauty."

For several moments utter silence filled the room even as the light filled it. Seeker almost feared to shatter it, but finally spoke as quietly as it could. "Thassyil tells me the city provides the Vyinnlyirr with everything."

"Indeed it does," the Leader said musingly. "Everything. Food, water, heat, air, life, happiness, entertainment, learning, beauty. Everything."

"Then why do you need a Questioner?"

The Leader turned and looked at Seeker for several moments. Then it turned back to the window and sighed. "Ah, the light, the light is so beautiful! See how it flows and..."

A flicker. A brief quiver. A microsecond of darkness. And then everything was as before.

"What... what was that?" Seeker stuttered in shock.

"That? Ah, you refer to the flicker? Oh, nothing, nothing. Just a shift of the generators or something like that. It means nothing. Don't be concerned. Look at the light instead. Look."

How often does that happen? Seeker demanded of Thassyil.

How often? Thassyil responded. Oh, flickers are rare. Maybe one or two a week, that's all.

What do they mean? Seeker pressed.

Nothing, Thassyil declared, its mind suddenly furtive. They mean nothing at all. A mere shifting of the generators or something. Nothing more than that.

Perhaps, Seeker thought, shielding its mind from its host, perhaps I am coming closer to my answer.

III.

The room which held the Sender was indeed impressive. It was perched atop a tower that stretched higher than any Seeker had entered so far. The room was roughly circular and the wall was thin and transparent. As a result, the view across the city was spectacular. The city of the Vyinnlyirr was vaster than Seeker had realized. The towers and the arching bridges that connected them tumbled off in every direction in what appeared to Seeker's eyes a brilliant chaos. They reminded the Novice of nothing so much as handfuls of jewels thrown at random, piling one on top of the other by sheer chance. Or perhaps, Seeker thought, trying somehow to encompass the experience of the city, it was as if a million rainbows had collided and as the light and color shattered and fell to the ground, they solidified and froze into these soaring towers of crystal.

When Seeker raised its three eyes from the city view to gaze overhead, it noticed something odd. At first the Novice simply stared, uncomprehending. Then slowly, awestruck, it realized what it was looking at. The entire city was covered by a vast, transparent dome. Seeker did some quick estimates. The dome had to be a good mile high at its apex and perhaps ten miles across. The weight of such a thing had to be stupendous, and the stresses on it almost beyond belief. Yet it appeared to be all of one piece of the same thin substance the rest of the city was constructed of. There was no way of even guessing what the dome could be made of. Nothing in Seeker's experience could be so thin, so transparent, and so immensely strong. It appears to be fragile crystal, but obviously it can't be, Seeker realized. It must be some material they've created, some incredible substance that their superior technology has discovered.

Finally satiated by the view, Seeker turned back into the room and studied the Sender. For a long time, the Novice walked around and around the Sender, examining it carefully. Finally the creature stopped and sighed deeply. It no longer doubted the superiority of the Vyinnlyirr's technology. The Sender alone was proof of it. The machine was one vast crystal, pulsing with light. The Novice could see no working, moving parts at all. Obviously the Sender had thrown out a signal, but Seeker couldn't even begin to fathom how.

Thassyil was absolutely no help. The host either didn't know or was hiding whatever information it had. Thassyil had readily shown Seeker the way to the Sender. But then the Vyinnlyirr had retreated behind a wall of silence and refused to answer any direct questions with direct answers.

As Seeker stood and gazed into the crystalline distances with ever-growing awe and bafflement, it heard a slight noise behind it, as if someone had entered the room of the Sender through its opening. Seeker turned slowly and beheld a Vyinnlyirr it had never seen before. The creature was strikingly different from Thryimm, Syssyir, the Leader or the Keeper of Memories. It was shorter, duller, with rather shabby looking membranes. Its eyes darted furtively around the room as if looking for a lurking enemy. "Hsssst," it whispered suddenly, "are you alone?"

"Yes. That is, except for Thassyil."

The creature whistled a sardonic trill. "Thassyil! Ha! You might as well be alone as with that moron! But there are none of the others with you? Not Thryimm?"

"No," Seeker said, wondering at this Vyinnlyirr's nervous attitude. "I came here quite alone. I needed to think."

"Huh. I shouldn't wonder. What trash have they told you so far? Did they say anything about the flickers, eh, eh?"

"Just that they are common and nothing to worry about. I

City of Crystal Shadow 33

imagine it's just a simple shifting of generators or something of that sort."

"Common," the strange Vyinnlyirr hissed, "oh, indeed, common! More and more common with each passing year! But not just nothing to worry about, oh, no, not that at all. They're fools, the whole lot of them. It's right there before their three eyes and they refuse to see it."

"What's right there?" Seeker asked, suddenly excited by the bizarre visitation. Perhaps this Vyinnlyirr knew something about the Call and why it had been made!

The creature's glance became sly and furtive again. It hopped sideways and cocked its head to one side, glancing at Seeker from the side of one eye. "Right there, it is, right at the end of their beaks. Yes, the flickers, yes, right there. Oh, they mean something, they do."

"What?" Seeker asked, filled with eager anticipation. "What do they mean?"

The strange Vyinnlyirr took two quick steps back and blinked at Seeker. The eyes on either side of its beak narrowed while its third eye closed completely. "And the Others, have they told you about the Others?"

The Novice started. "Others? What are you talking about? What Others?" A vague sense of confusion and concern rose up from Thassyil's mind. Seeker noted it with interest and then ignored it to concentrate on the stranger. I'll try to question my host later, it decided, though I doubt I'll get much satisfaction. Why, it wondered briefly, had they given a Questioner such an ignorant host? Surely a more knowledgeable host would have been able to aid in the investigation. It didn't make sense. Or was it purposeful? Filing the question away for later consideration, Seeker turned its attention back to the stranger. "What Others?"

"Oh, for certain they wouldn't tell you about the Others! Oh, no, not them. They want to hide the fact that the Others even exist at all! Keep it hidden, keep it from the light, that's what they want. Yes, yes. Ask them about the Others!" The creature suddenly hunched down and swung its head in wary circles, glancing wildly about it at the alarmingly revealing walls. "There's no hiding here. The light comes in everywhere, everywhere," the stranger muttered. Then it looked directly at Seeker, its eyes suddenly wild and filled with anger. "Yes, ask them what happens to those who can't fit into the Project, to those who can't stand the light!" It whirled suddenly and before Seeker had a chance to stop it, the stranger disappeared through the opening.

Thryimm shook its head fretfully. "Others? What Others are you talking about? There are no Others here in our city. There are only the Vyinnlyirr, the Children of Light and Air. Who have you been talking to, Questioner?"

"I . . . I don't really know. A Vyinnlyirr, I assume, though not a very impressive specimen, I admit. It . . ." Seeker paused, suddenly cautious, warned in some subtle way by Thryimm's posture, by the tilt of the creature's head. Labyrinth taught me to be careful, Seeker thought, honed my senses to danger. There is danger in this room. I don't have to be H*mb*1 to feel the heavy beat of its presence.

"Yes?" Thryimm encouraged. "It what?"

"It seemed strange, foolish. Or perhaps I misunderstood. I'm still so new here, I . . ."

"True," Thryimm answered too quickly, too ready to accept the excuse. "True, you probably misunderstood. Our language is a subtle one and it will take time to master. Yes, that must be it."

"What is it like outside the city, Thryimm?" Seeker asked to change the topic.

"Wasteland. Hot, arid, deadly. Filled with poisonous vapors that sear the lungs and cloud the eye. Life there is impossible for the Vyinnlyirr."

"But once you lived there, didn't you? I mean, before you built the city?"

"No. We never lived there. No. Once it could have supported life, though it was a poor place to begin with. But it took this entire world, all of its resources, everything, to build this city. What's left is a lifeless desert. Nothing lives there now. Nothing. Nothing."

"But I thought the Leader said there were some lizards and things. I mean, there is some life, right?"

"Lizards, yes. Insects, yes. But no real life. No Children of Light and Air. No Vyinnlyirr. The very air is poisonous. Impossible to breathe for long. It burns the lungs, makes the eyes water and cloud over. And there is no water and nothing to eat. No real life can live there. No Vyinnlyirr."

The vehemence of Thryimm's denials surprised Seeker and

made the Novice wonder. "Is that why there is a dome over the city? To keep the bad air out?"

"Yes! Yes, that is why there is a dome. To keep the bad air out and the sweet air and moisture in. Yes. The dome is only for that reason. Not for any other. We need no protection, you see, from anything but the bad air."

"Would it be possible to go out on the surface? Only for a little while, of course. Just to see it firsthand."

Thryimm looked startled. Its head jerked from side to side and it opened its beak wide several times. "Outside?" its voice came out in a strangled squeak. "Outside into the waste? No, no, no such thing is possible!"

"Do you mean there is no way out, no opening or anything?"

The Vyinnlyirr glanced worriedly at Seeker. "Opening? Opening to the outside? No. There is no opening. Why would we want an opening to the outside? The city cares for all our needs. It gives the Vyinnlyirr everything we need. There is nothing we need from the outside. We took all we need from there thousands of years ago. There is nothing there now, nothing!"

A sudden flicker. The light shifted, darker, duller. The continual sigh of moving air halted. A ringing groan came from the crystal. Thassyil moaned and shuddered in Seeker's mind. Then everything was back to normal. "What was that?" Seeker asked.

"Nothing important," Thryimm declared, its eyes flicking back and forth in confused fear. "Nothing. Just a flicker. They happen from time to time, but it means nothing."

" 'Nothing' seems to be everyone's favorite word around here," Seeker muttered sarcastically. "Flickers mean nothing. Nothing lives outside. Nothing is wrong. Nothing."

"I must go now," Thryimm said, suddenly eager to leave. "I must go to meet with the Leader. The Leader will send for you soon and then you can ask the Leader any questions you may have."

"Yes," Seeker muttered as Thryimm turned and stepped through the opening. "I may ask questions. I just don't seem to be allowed to receive any answers!"

I'm hungry, Thassyil grumbled sullenly in Seeker's mind. The Novice stopped its pacing. "Hungry?" it replied out loud. "Ah, yes, I suppose even the Children of Light and Air live on something solider. Hmmmm. Where does a Vyinnlyirr go to get fed around here?"

"The blue place over there on the wall. Touch it, and it will open to reveal food. The city puts it there. It is there right now."

"Ah, yes, I see it. I remember now. We ate from there once before." Seeker stepped over to the spot and reached out its hand. Just short of the blue area it stopped. "Are you very hungry, Thassyil?"

"Yes. You have been in my mind for three feeding periods and have eaten only once. I have been, uh, unaware for a good part of that time. But now I realize how hungry I am."

Seeker dropped its hand and took a step back from the blue area. It too felt the sudden surge of hunger in its Vyinnlyirr body. Yes, Thassyil was indeed hungry and so am I, it realized. But...

"Why are you not opening the blue area, Questioner?" Thassyil whined. "Please. Let us eat."

"Ah, yes, eat. Hmmmm. Thassyil, tell me about the Others and then we can eat."

"Others?" Thassyil's response was a frightened squawk. The host's mind collapsed back into itself in sudden confusion and fear. "Others? I don't know anything about any Others. Nothing. There are only Vyinnlyirr here in the city. No Others."

"Then if the Others are not here in the city, where are they? Outside in the waste? Are there Others in the waste, Thassyil?" Seeker pressed its host.

"No! No, there is nothing in the waste! Nothing!" Thassyil sounded panicky. The host's fear swelled suddenly and threatened to inundate Seeker's own mind. "Nothing! There is nothing in the waste! That one in the tower lied to you! No Others! There are no Others!" Thassyil's panic waned almost as rapidly as it had waxed. Its thoughts were suddenly weak and disjointed. "Hungry. Questioner. Nice to feed. No Others. Please feed. No. Waste empty. Nothing. Feed." Its tone became whimpering and plaintive.

Seeker sighed with frustration. Damn! Why have they given me such a moron for a host? Thassyil may have the most beautiful membranes in the whole city, but it is a fool. "All right." Seeker relented and stepped to the blue area. It touched the wall, the crystal warm and almost soft to the touch. A portion of the wall slid back to reveal a cavity in which a small bowl rested. The bowl, of blue crystal, was filled with small pellets. Seeker felt a sudden surge of hunger and lifted the bowl to its beak. With a few quick pecks, it devoured the pellets. In the back of its mind, quiet at last, the Novice heard Thassyil mumble contentedly.

Why such a fool? Seeker asked itself again. Or *is* Thassyil a fool? Perhaps Thassyil was actually the norm for the Vyinnlyirr. Perhaps even one of the bright ones. But that seemed improbable. After all, the city pointed to a very advanced race, one with a very sophisticated technology, one that could . . .

A sudden idea stopped Seeker short. The city was very old. It had been built thousands of years ago. The creatures who had built the city had clearly been a superior culture. But that didn't necessarily mean that their descendants, thousands of years later, would still maintain the same high level. Could it be that the Vyinnlyirr were the degenerate remnants of a once brilliant race? That they lived like foolish children in a wonderland built by long-gone adults?

The flickers! Could they be a symptom of something? What if the descendants of the city's builders were no longer capable of even maintaining the city? What if the technology had been lost to a point where everything was coming apart and no one knew how to fix it any more? Could the flickers be symptoms of the system's gradual breakdown? Perhaps the Call had been made to get help in keeping the city alive.

But if that was the case, why was everybody denying that the flickers meant anything, that they were routine? It made no sense. The flickers seemed to indicate something was wrong. Seeker was there to find out what was wrong and try to help set it right. But no one would admit that the flickers were anything wrong.

Except the stranger. The stranger had hinted they were indeed a sign of a breakdown. Or something. And the Others. Thassyil clearly knew something, but was afraid to even discuss it. The fear was a strange one, too, Seeker realized. Not just a fear of making Thryimm or the Leader or some other authority angry. No, it was an internal fear, a deep-seated dread that came from inside rather than being imposed from without. Thassyil was not afraid someone would find out it had talked about the Others. It was afraid of the very idea of the Others! Its fear was below the conscious level.

Seeker made up its mind. "Thassyil," it demanded in a tone that brooked no disagreement, "I want to see the Keeper of Memories again. Take me to its nest. Now."

The Keeper of Memories blinked and turned its head quizzically to one side. "Others? Others?"

"Yes," Seeker responded encouragingly. "Have you any memories of Others?"

"Hmmmmmm, hmmmmm, Others. Yes, yes, but they go back, back to a time before the city. They are dim and shadowy, uncertain, almost mythical. Soft memories that could never do as hard data, that could never be depended on for making decisions."

"Tell me," Seeker asked gently. "Please tell me anyway."

The Keeper of Memories trilled a tired sigh. "Ah, ah, so far back. It is the dim dawn time when nothing is clear and all blends together in one shadowy whole. There were Others in the air and on the ground. There was fire and death, falling from the sky, smashing into hard earth. Shattered limbs. A dying. Cries of pain. Torn and ruined membranes. A striking downward. Running prey, scattering it all directions, but fighting, killing even as it is killed. A dying. Torn and ruined membranes. Nests ripped and pulled down.

"Then a victory, small, limited, but turning the tide. Hunting the Others down. Seeking them out, driving them from their lairs, killing, exterminating. Nest robbers, egg breakers, membrane destroyers, shattered, scattered, humbled, savaged, harried, decimated. Extinguished. Extinct." The Keeper of Memories fell silent for several moments. Then it whistled sadly, mournfully. "Long and long ago it was. Memory reaches back but cannot arrive there. Too long ago. Dim, too dim for the light of the mind to shine and reveal. It comes not forth, but recedes as one approaches. It seeks the dark when one brings the light. There is no way to it, no clearer view. I cannot do more for you, Questioner. There are no other memories."

Seeker shook itself, dragging its own mind back from the shadowy memories that had all but overwhelmed it. The words of the Keeper of Memories had thrown it back into its own memories, memories buried deep in the unconscious mind, vague, unformed, chaotic. Seeker had suddenly found itself in a time of swirling fear and uncertainty, a time when the Vyinnlyirr had fought for existence against other species on its planet, fought for supremacy and the right to survive. The two suns had cast strange shadows and had...

The Novice's reminiscence came to a sudden halt. Its memories had been of two suns. Two. There was only one in the sky of this planet. One single blue star. Not two, one huge and red, the other tiny and white.

The realization was sudden, total and stunning. This was not the planet the Vyinnlyirr had evolved on! This was not their home world! Sometime, long ago, the Vyinnlyirr had come here to this system from another one. They had invaded this planet. The Vyinnlyirr were alien invaders!

IV.

"Invaders?" Thryimm trilled with amusement. "I would hardly call the Vyinnlyirr invaders. It is true we have confused memories of defeating other species, both those of the air and those of the earth, which once competed with us for dominance. But I fail to see that that makes us invaders."

"Thryimm," Seeker said firmly, "the planet you gained dominance of was not this planet."

Thryimm's trill was louder and more hilarious. "Not this planet? What an absurd idea! We have always been here. This is our home world, Questioner. What could ever possess you to . . ."

"The memories in Thassyil's mind are of a planet with two suns," Seeker interrupted harshly. "Look upward, Thryimm. This system is a single star system, not a double. Your original world, the world of your racial memories, had two stars, a red giant and a white dwarf. I know, Thryimm. I've seen."

Thryimm stared silently at Seeker for several moments. Then the Vyinnlyirr nodded its head slowly, its third eye blinking rapidly. "Yes, yes, you have seen. If you can delve that deeply into Thassyil's racial memories, you have gained a greater control over its mind than we thought possible. Much greater. I thought that such use of the host's mind was considered improper for a Questioner." Thryimm's tone was cold and slightly hostile.

"I have never forced Thassyil to reveal anything," Seeker replied calmly. "I have taken what has been freely given. There is nothing wrong in that. But I have not invaded my host's mind, nor have I ever pried or thrust my way inside."

Thryimm sighed. "I knew we should have picked a stronger host. Thassyil has magnificent membranes and we wanted to honor the Questioner most highly. But a stronger mind would have been better. Thassyil is . . . vulnerable, weak, foolish."

Thryimm gazed wordlessly, thoughtfully at Seeker and nodded slightly as if reaching a decision. "Yes, we came here from our original world. About fifty-three thousand years ago. Double star systems are not particularly stable, and planetary orbits in them are erratic at best. For a thousand years the temperatures are fine. Then for the next thousand they are far too warm for comfort. And then they become too cold. The cycle is difficult to survive, let alone to develop sentience in.

"It was a miracle we became a sentient race. A miracle. It was probably the conflict between the five major species on our planet that catapulted us into intelligence. Sentience gave us the edge we needed to win the war for survival against the other four. At least one of them, a ground species, also had developed a modicum of intelligence. They were our most bitter opponents. We almost destroyed each other. You can check with Thassyil for the accuracy of all this. It's all in Thassyil's memory.

"We triumphed. And the turbulence of the environment of a planet in a double star system gave us plenty of opportunity to sharpen our wits. We became larger, first gliding rather than flying, then became altogether earthbound as our planet entered a cold phase. We almost perished, but once again our intelligence saved us.

"As we had conquered our enemies, we conquered our environment. We learned to deal with the cold. Then the hot cycle came and nearly destroyed us once again. Once more we triumphed.

"Each time we lost a little ground and gained a lot. Slowly, slowly, we pulled ahead. We developed a civilization, a technology. . . .

"We knew the system was going critical long before it actually happened. We were ready. We left and came here. Here in another system." Thryimm looked skyward. "At night, if the light were dimmed, you would be able to see our old home system. The gas ball from the explosion is still expanding. It's a very beautiful sight. Eventually the shock wave will reach this system and then it will not be so beautiful.

"Yes, Questioner, we came here, but hardly as invaders. Refugees is more like it. Refugees on a desolate, barely habitable world. There was nothing here to invade, you see. Nothing but the poisonous lizards and the harsh air.

"But once again we had to fight, Questioner. We fought and defeated this barren, harsh environment and built this." Thryimm took in the whole city with a sweeping gesture. "The city, the embodiment of the spirit of the Children of Light and Air."

Thryimm fixed Seeker with a hard stare from all three of its eyes. "Does that answer your question? Is there anything else I can tell you?"

Seeker sensed the arrogant edge in Thryimm's voice and wondered at it. The Vyinnlyirr acted as if it had just won some kind of victory. What could that mean? This was clearly no time to press the issue. Seeker had learned a great deal and needed time to digest and understand the significance of all it had been told. How much was true and how much invention?

"No," the Novice said mildly, "no, that's fine. For the moment, that's fine."

The hardness of the gleam in Thryimm's eye as it turned away was unmistakable.

Syssyir looked uncomfortable. "It's possible, yes. Indeed, I do believe I have some such memories. But they aren't readily accessible, Questioner, you must realize that. Generally we can't tap such deep memories except in the presence of the Keeper of Memories. And even then, not everyone has memories of the same strength or clarity. Perhaps Thassyil has such strong memories to compensate for, ummm, a somewhat weak intellect."

"So then you think the Others the stranger referred to are simply the species you exterminated on your rise to dominance on your home planet?"

Syssyir fluttered its membranes. "What else?"

"Well, for one, perhaps a species native to this planet which was destroyed when you came here. Perhaps a sentient species you destroyed when you invaded."

The other Vyinnlyirr trilled nervously. "But I've never heard of such a thing. I have no such memories."

"They'd be old ones. Perhaps just as hard to get hold of as those from the home world. Perhaps even harder, if they were blocked in some way." Seeker stalked back and forth in moody silence. "Look, Syssyir, the Keeper of Memories leapt immediately into the distant past in response to my question. Why did it go back that far?"

"But, if the Others are simply those ancient species..."

Seeker interrupted with a derisive trill. " 'If,' oh yes, 'if.' But that is precisely the problem."

"It makes sense. It happened. It..."

"It makes sense, yes. Too much sense. But it doesn't seem likely that the stranger would warn me to ask about something that took place a million years ago on a different planet in a different system. That doesn't make sense."

"Maybe," Syssyir said slowly, "the stranger was lying."

Seeker stopped dead in its tracks and turned to face Syssyir. "Lying? But, why would..."

Syssyir fluttered its membranes again. "Why would Thryimm lie? Or the Keeper of Memories? You seem quite ready to assume they are lying. Why not give this strange Vyinnlyirr the benefit of the same doubt?"

Seeker gave Syssyir a long, considering look. An idea had just crossed the Novice's mind. "Syssyir, do you know all of the Vyinnlyirr?"

"All of the Vyinnlyirr? Well, not all, but probably most. At least those that dwell in this area of the city. I might not know some who live on the fringes toward the sunrise."

"Do you know the one I described, the stranger?"

Syssyir's third eye blinked rapidly and the other two took on a furtive look. "The stranger? No. Why, no. I don't ummmm, recognize the Vyinnlyirr you described. It must come from the fringes, from someplace..."

"Why are you lying?" Seeker asked softly.

"Lying?" Syssyir's voice was a squawk. It shut its third eye tightly. "Why do you think I'm lying? I really..."

Without waiting to hear the rest of the sentence, Seeker turned and strode from the room.

* * *

The Novice walked the sparkling streets and delicate bridges of the city, passing from gleaming tower to glowing spire across the yawning, light-filled spaces between them. It walked with its head down, deep in concentration, mulling over the strange and contradictory information it had gathered. The few Vyinnlyirr it met turned quickly aside as if surprised and frightened. Seeker failed to even notice them.

Its mind drifted back, back to that day when it had stood on the Plain and gazed in awe at the place where the ground rose up and up and up to meet the sky. That day, chasing the springdasher across a vast carpet of white flowers, it had stumbled on a mystery, a vast, incomprehensible mystery which had driven it from one disaster to another throughout its life. As a Chaser, as a Catcher, even as a Nurturer, the mystery of the Plain rising up to meet the sky had haunted and hounded Seeker, had driven it to seek answers where none were allowed. The mystery had changed the mind and the life of the Chaser called Swift for all time.

It was at that exact moment, Seeker suddenly realized, that I truly became Seeker. It was many years before I finally took that name, but it was that discovery which led step by step, with sure inevitability to the point where I am now.

And where am I now? Faced with another mystery. Another mystery that could change my life just as surely as that first one. If I had any brains, I'd go back to the ship right now and get out of here. Just like I should have forgotten that I ever saw the Plain rising into the clouds. Seeker chuckled silently. Fat chance! I'm just not made that way. I'm Seeker and that's all there is to it. And besides, I'm a Questioner now. I have a duty. A duty to the universe. But especially to those others who were there on Labyrinth with me. Those who tried and failed. To Darkhider and Thisunit. And to H*mb*l. Yes, most of all to H*mb*l.

But there is something very strange here. Strange and wrong. And perhaps very, very dangerous. Seeker's senses, heightened by its experiences on Labyrinth, where even the slightest thing could mean instant, brutal death, were on full alert. Something, something, hung vaguely, a dim shadow of menace, behind everything Seeker saw and heard here in this city of crystal light and shadow.

They are lying to me, all of them, Seeker knew. But I don't know which part of what they are saying is a lie and which

City of Crystal Shadow

the truth. And even more importantly, I don't know why they are lying.

It was several moments before Seeker realized that a Vyinnlyirr was walking silently by its side. It glanced out of the side of one of its eyes and saw that the creature keeping pace with it was about as tall as its host, with a fine set of membranes. Its coloring was somewhat duller than Thassyil's, but it looked healthy and strong.

Yet when it turned its head to meet Seeker's gaze, the Novice was stunned to see that both of its large eyes were clouded and dull. Blind! Seeker realized instantly. Thassyil recoiled with repugnance and quickly retreated deep into solitude.

The blind Vyinnlyirr nodded slightly. "That is correct, Questioner. I am mostly blind. I have only one eye to see from, the one that senses only the lower wavelengths. I can 'see' you only as a heat source, a warm spot against a cool background. The city, the glorious personification of the spirit of the Children of Light and Air is mostly invisible to me." Its voice held a bitter edge, but the bitterness was weary, as if long accepted and grown used to.

"I am called Seeker. And you?"

"Lissyi, the Blind One. I have been this way since birth. I have never seen the city as you see it now. Pity me, Seeker." Lissyi's voice had fallen to an angry hiss.

"I had no idea there were blind Vyinnlyirr. Surely with all this wonderful technology, your people should be able to . . ."

Lissyi's harsh trill caused Seeker's words to die in its throat. "Wonderful technology! Oh, indeed wonderful! Ancient, wonderful . . . and forgotten! Don't you realize by now, Questioner, that we live like prisoners in this Crystal City? Prisoners who know nothing of how to run things. Prisoners who watch helplessly, hopelessly as the city slowly, slowly, but surely disintegrates and dies around us." Lissyi gestured grandly at the city. "This wonder, this glory, this personification of the spirit of our race which I cannot see, this city is dying! And we are dying with it!"

Seeker felt a thrill of discovery. "Is that why the Call was made, Lissyi? Did you make it?"

Lissyi trilled sardonically. "The Call? No, I did not make the Call. Nor did any of those like me. We have no access to the Sender. No. The Call was made for other reasons. Other reasons. The city is dying. We are dying. But that is not why the Call was made. Ask the Leader why the Call was made. Do not ask me!"

With that, Lissyi turned abruptly and swiftly strode off down a narrow street. It stopped after a few steps and whirled back to face Seeker. "Go down to the base of the city, Questioner. See for yourself what it is like at ground level. It is dying, decaying, falling into ruin. And our soaring spirit, the spirit of the Children of Light and Air, is falling into ruin with it!"

A moment later, Seeker stood alone with the beautiful light shimmering serenely around it.

V.

The Leader nodded solemnly. "Ah, Questioner, you could have saved yourself a lot of wasted time if you had come directly to me with your question. Hmmmm, yes, wasted time. But, no matter. Time is not of the essence. Only the question counts.

"So. The Others. A myth. We came here, long, long ago, from a world that was dying. We found a savage race here, barely sentient. We tried, as is fitting for a fully sentient race, to raise them to the light. But the task was doomed to failure, I fear. They were a recalcitrant lot, refusing to serve apprenticeship in order to climb out of the slough of ignorance they wallowed in. They had no wings, either physically or metaphorically, on which to soar. We tried, ah, how we tried.

"Their world was a poor one to begin with, and as we began to build the city, it became progressively poorer. All the resources of this planet, including even the water and air, were needed for our great task. The environment outside the city deteriorated in direct proportion as that within it improved.

"The native species of this world refused to join us in the city. We promised them positions of honor, helping us to run and maintain the machinery that keeps the city functioning. But they stubbornly refused. Eventually, we closed the city off from the outside world entirely and shut them out permanently."

The Leader paused and sighed deeply. "It was a sad day, for their fate was inevitable. Some of the less complex species on this planet managed to adapt over time to the new circumstances created by the construction of the city. Some were already prepared for such conditions. But the majority could not change sufficiently to survive. The native semisentients were one of the species that failed. They died out some fifteen thousand years ago.

"Now nothing sentient roams the waste. I will ask to have you provided with a bestiary listing and displaying pictures of all the creatures that still survive on the surface. The number doesn't exceed two dozen."

Seeker gazed thoughtfully at the Leader. "So the Others are merely a myth?"

The Leader nodded. "Yes. Some of the Vyinnlyirr still harbor a sense of guilt over the fate of that unfortunate species. They would, I think, like to believe that somewhere, deep within the wastes, they still exist. You see, Questioner, we are a gentle species, mostly given to the wonders of the mind. The very idea of having been the cause, however indirect, of the extinction of a sentient species gives us great anguish. Hence the foolish myth—or should I say foolish wish?—that somewhere, somehow, these sad victims still exist and still have hope."

Plausible, Seeker thought, entirely plausible. And yet somehow wrong. In some way the whole story had a false ring to it. The rhythm was slightly off beat, the melody off key. H*mb*l would feel it immediately and understand it. I can sense it, but not uncover it. There is danger here. This lie hides something the Vyinnlyirr don't want known. What?

"You're absolutely sure there are no survivors?" Seeker asked. "Have you searched for them?"

The Leader nodded slowly. "Absolutely sure. We searched many, many times. Oh, that was long, long ago. Ten thousand years at least. Oh, yes, and then again about six thousand years ago. Both times the results were negative. There is no sign, no evidence. Nothing."

"And yet the myth of the Others persists."

"Yes. The guilt must be great. It has been six thousand years since we even noticed anything outside our City, twenty thou-

City of Crystal Shadow

sand since we even lived outside it. And still we feel a sadness over the fate of these creatures. It may seem foolish of us, Questioner, but it is a harmless foolishness, one of compassion that can easily be forgiven, no?"

Seeker turned and gestured at the city. "Twenty thousand years since you entered your great city of crystal. Six thousand since you've looked at anything outside it or even deigned to notice the rest of the planet. And what have you done in all that time? What do the Vyinnlyirr do? I see nothing happening. I barely even see any Vyinnlyirr."

The Leader pulled itself taller, more erect. Its pose became one of pride. "What do we do? Ah, Questioner, that is truly the most important question of all! What do the Vyinnlyirr do in their city of light and air?" The Leader turned suddenly and gestured to Seeker. "Come with me. It is indeed time to show you what the Vyinnlyirr do."

Seeker followed the Leader to an opening at the far end of the hall. The two of them passed through and found themselves on an arching bridge that soared effortlessly across open spaces like a scarlet rainbow shot with glints of yellow and green. At its far end, they entered a huge tower that rose almost to the dome.

Inside the tower they climbed up and up and up until they stood at last in a vast room, high above the city. The room was bathed in a cool blue light that sparkled and shimmered with an icy joy. Seeker felt soothed and excited at the same time.

The Leader stopped in the center of the room and gestured grandly around. "This," it said with overflowing pride, "is what the Vyinnlyirr do. This is the Project."

The Novice gazed around in confusion. The room was empty except for a few low tables and the blue light that slowly swirled through it. "The Project?" Seeker asked, realizing it sounded slow and stupid.

The Leader trilled happily, in high good humor. "Yes! This is the center of the Project, the place where it all comes together. You might call it the Control Room, though the idea that anyone or anything controls the Project is ludicrous.

"The Project!" the Leader trilled in ecstacy. "The greatest endeavor of sentient life in the entire universe!" It cocked its head to one side and fixed Seeker with a fervent stare. "You will be the first outside the Vyinnlyirr to hear of it, Questioner!

The very first!" The Leader began to stalk back and forth across the room, all the while speaking quickly and excitedly.

"The Project commenced back on our home planet, over sixty thousand years ago. It was then that we began to investigate, to examine, to try to understand the ultimate mystery of the universe. Oh, don't shrink back in dismay! We are not such fools as to think we can uncover the wonder of the whole universe. No, no! Such a thing is not even necessary.

"No, indeed, our Project is much simpler, much grander than that! Yes, yes! The mystery we sought to understand, the tangled knot we sought to unravel, the abyss we determined to plumb was simply ourselves. For we realized that to know ourselves, the Vyinnlyirr, the Children of Light and Air, fully and totally, was to see into the very heart of the mystery of the universe itself. For the microcosm and the macrocosm are one! It is a unity!

"But you step back in wonder! You shake your head in disbelief! And well you might, well you might. For you can see easily that we were seeking nothing less than knowledge of Being itself, of the Thing-in-Itself, of Existence as such.

"Ordinary knowledge was not enough for us. The world of appearance was not sufficient. It is a real world, oh, yes. It must exist in some sense. But that sense is fluctuating, imperfect, shifting from perspective to perspective. You see the city now through the eyes of the Vyinnlyirr. Had you your own eyes, it would appear vastly different. The things that appear to us through the medium of our senses vary according to the nature and quality of those senses. Some species sense one thing, others another. How different does the universe look to a species that sees only in the ultraviolet from the way it seems to one that sees only the infrared! And that is but a minor example, for the senses extend far beyond the electromagnetic spectrum. Think of the senses of the arachnids!

"No, the world of the senses, the world we call that of appearance, is a shifting thing, unsure, indeterminate. And there is no way of ever encompassing it entirely. For there is no end to it, no way to collect enough viewpoints of it to contain it. It spills over any box we try to put it in.

"Then how is knowledge possible? Ah, that is a key question! If the world of appearance is so uncertain, how can we ever say we know anything? How can we claim that our knowledge, so grand and proud, is anything but a hollow gesture subject to change at every moment?

"What if we strip away everything we get from our senses?" The Leader picked a blue crystal from a low table and held it out to Seeker. "What if we took away the color of this crystal, its shine, its glow? What if we took away its form, its mass, its solidity? What have we left? Why, the space it exists in! And the time in which it exists!

"Think of it, Questioner! If we take everything away, we are left with two things! Space and time! It is possible to think of a space emptied of all things and even of empty time. But it is not possible to think of the nonexistence of either time or space! They are primary!

"Where do they come from? Do they exist as such? But that can't be! For if they do, then they are things, just like other things, and could be thought away in the same fashion. And worse yet, if space is a thing, then there must be a space for it to exist in. And a space for that space, and so on in an infinite regression. The same would hold for time. No. No, they must be something else. But what?

"Ah, they are the very fabric of our minds, the very stuff sentience is made of, Questioner! They are the very way in which we make the universe visible and experienceable to ourselves as sentients. They are the rules we set up, the concepts that make sensing possible. We create them, for without them the universe is impossible for us.

"And that means they come *before* experience, that they are the very framework within which things can at all appear to us so that experience is possible!"

The Leader stopped and stared at Seeker, its three eyes ablaze, its membrane flaring out in display. "But time and space are not the only things that come from within us, Questioner. Oh, no! They are the things that relate to our senses. But there is more that we create before experience, things that come directly from our faculty of understanding. Yes! Think of concepts like cause and effect! Think of mathematics! And there are more, many more! And none of them come from experience, but rather make experience itself possible.

"We do not come to the universe like empty vessels, waiting to be filled. We come with a structure, a way of seeing and understanding already built in!

"But does that get us any closer to the real world, the world of Being and Things-in-Themselves that stand, hidden, behind appearance? Is there any way to rip apart the curtain of appearance and get to the reality itself? Is there a path that leads to the direct knowledge of the Thing-in-Itself, reality stripped of the structure we place on it?

"If it lies anywhere, Questioner, it lies within us! Within us as it does within every sentient species! But only the Vyinnlyirr have realized this truth! Only the Vyinnlyirr have realized it and dedicated themselves to penetrating to the very core of this problem!

"That, Questioner, is the Project! The attempt to totally and utterly plumb the meaning and very being of ourselves. For when we can completely explain ourselves, we will be in reality explaining the entire universe!"

The Leader gestured around the room again. "This is the center of it all. The center of this whole city. For that is what the city is, Questioner. The city is the Project. The city is a vast collection of every fact, every thought, every nuance, every meaning, every hint, of the Vyinnlyirr. The city is the Vyinnlyirr, our spirit, our meaning, our existence. It cares for us, providing for our every need so we can be free, utterly free to concentrate on the Project. The city makes us free to do that which must be done, for that is the only true freedom!

"Here in our city of light and air we correlate, compare, separate, examine everything, working toward that day when it is all complete. On that day the Vyinnlyirr will have accomplished the greatest triumph in the history of sentience! We will understand ourselves. And thereby understand the universe!"

Seeker stood and stared about the empty room with a mixture of awe and fear. It occurred to the Novice that the Vyinnlyirr were mad. And it was inextricably caught up in their madness.

Back in Thassyil's quarters, Seeker pondered what it had seen and heard. Is it possible that the Vyinnlyirr are mad? it wondered. Every bit as crazy as Thisunit and its race? Thisunit's people had been seeking some kind of encyclopedic knowledge, too. That was why they had sent unit after unit to Labyrinth. The planet had been an anomaly in their scheme and they had been trying to understand it. Thisunit had failed in the same way all the units before it had failed. There simply was no way to fit Labyrinth into a nice, neat, rational scheme.

City of Crystal Shadow

But surely what the Vyinnlyirr were engaged in was saner than that, Seeker reasoned. They sought only self-understanding, a total and exhaustive cataloguing of every aspect of their own being. Wasn't that a possible thing to accomplish? Seeker didn't know exactly why, but it was sure the Vyinnlyirr's goal was just as insanely unattainable as Thisunit's.

So the city was nothing more than a vast Project? Then what did that make the Vyinnlyirr within its dome? The answer was clear and disturbing. They were the subjects the Project was studying. They were just laboratory animals, just parts of a vast experiment.

A sudden suspicion bloomed in Seeker's mind. Was any of this true? Or was it all just another mask the Vyinnlyirr were hiding behind? The Leader had seemed sincere enough, but where was the proof? The whole thing could just as easily be a tissue of lies. But why? Why lie? Or, more specifically and centrally, why call a Questioner down to the planet and then lie to it? What possible purpose could such an action have?

For a moment, Seeker's whirling thoughts almost overwhelmed it. Slow down, it told itself. Let's look at the options. First, the Leader is telling the truth. O.K. The Project is real. But then why call a Questioner? How could a Questioner help a race engaged in a project of self-examination? Try as hard as it could, the Novice could make no headway here.

Then try the alternative. The Leader was lying and the Project was a fake. Or if not a fake, then a diversion to steer the Questioner away from the truth. That meant that there was a truth, and that those facts were the real reason it had been Called. But then why steer it along so many false leads? What kind of game were the Vyinnlyirr playing and why?

Too many questions. Seeker shook a weary head. There's only one way to deal with a situation like this. Go a step at a time. Gather more information. Pile it up until a pattern of some kind appears. I don't have H*mb*l's instinctive feel for the flow and movement of things, the Novice admitted to itself. I'll just have to plod along at my own pace.

And yet my pace, slow and plodding as it is, got me across Labyrinth and to Sanctuary. While H*mb*l stays there, dancing with the death that lurks behind every stone, every leaf. Why? How can that be? H*mb*l goes to the core of things, surely, instinctively, while I stumble and flail around. Why did H*mb*l fail and I succeed? It makes no sense!

With a jerk, Seeker pulled its attention back to the present. No time to rummage around in the past, no matter how painful. Remember what it was like on Labyrinth. Inattention, even for a few seconds, could spell disaster. Death was always waiting in a hundred different guises. Just as it waits here in this city of light and air, here with these wonderfully rational Vyinnlyirr and their Project.

One step at a time. Take each problem, each little problem, and solve it. Only then will you be ready to grasp the big problem. Step by step.

What should the first step be? Seeker thought for several moments, then decided. A thorough exploration of the city, from top to bottom, was in order. Lissyi had indicated things could be learned by going down to the ground level. It was time to find out, time to see what the city consisted of. Perhaps, Seeker suddenly thought, even to get a glimpse of the outside.

Knowing the exploration would take a long time, Seeker went to the wall and touched the blue spot. It took the bowl of food and devoured it, even though it was not hungry yet. Then it ate another.

Finally ready, Seeker set off to explore.

VI.

It took the Novice many hours of searching to find its way down to what appeared to be ground level. Every time it tried to get Thassyil to give it information, the Vyinnlyirr host was evasive and unhelpful. It was only by trial and error that Seeker finally succeeded.

The ground on which it stood vibrated gently as if covering vast engines of power. Seeker scratched at it idly with Thassyil's claws. It seemed ordinary gravel and sand, very like that which must cover most of the surface of the planet. It seemed strange that the Vyinnlyirr left the native soil here at the base of their city. Why not cover the ground with the same crystal the rest of the city was made of?

The Novice walked slowly down a broad avenue between the bases of two towering buildings. There was no sign of other life, no Vyinnlyirr, no Others, nothing. Just that throbbing vibration from the ground and the gentle whisper of air.

And then it came. A low, growling roar. The ground began to vibrate more rapidly as if struggling to be free of something. It began to shake and heave, throwing up small puffs of dust and sand. Seeker could barely stay standing and staggered drunkenly toward one of the walls for support. The Novice felt Thassyil's sudden rising panic and clamped down hard on its host. There was a sudden thump, a groan, and a flicker of light that plunged Seeker into an instant of blackness. Then it was gone, and the hum continued as if it had never stopped, and the air glowed with serene light as it had for thousands of years.

"Now do you understand, Questioner?" Seeker spun around at the shock of the unexpected voice and found itself facing Lissyi, the blind Vyinnlyirr.

"How . . . how did you know I was here?"

"Only two of my eyes are blind, Questioner. And my mind is not blind at all. I knew you would come and knew there was only one way from where you stayed. When you passed I sensed you and followed. Now do you understand?"

"Understand what, Lissyi?"

"What I told you. Look about. Can you not see the ruin, the destruction? Is it not as I told you?"

Seeker looked around, confused. "I see no destruction, Lissyi, no degeneration. A bit of sand and gravel, but that's all."

Lissyi snorted. "Use your third eye. The one that sees in the long wavelengths. Look at the sand and gravel."

Cautiously, Seeker closed its two largest eyes and kept only the third one open. Instantly the world changed. Beneath the gravel, the Novice could see a floor of crystal, pitted and broken. And here and there, cracks appeared in the walls at the base of the towers that soared up on either side of the avenue. "The gravel," Seeker stammered, suddenly unsure of itself. "Where does it come from?"

"When the crystal degenerates, it turns back into gravel, the material it was originally made of," Lissyi answered. The blind Vyinnlyirr gestured vaguely around it. "All this gravel and sand isn't the original soil the city was built on. The city was built on crystal as a base. All of this is the result of crystal degenerating. Here at its base, the streets of the city are filled with it. That is why none of the Vyinnlyirr come here any longer. They fear what they see. For it spells the doom of the city of light and air."

"Doom?" Seeker asked slowly. "The city is doomed?"

"It will all crumble and turn to dust!" Lissyi cried out suddenly, jerking its arms wide. "Dust!"

"When?" Seeker asked, a sudden chill running through its mind.

"In twenty or thirty thousand years. It's hard to be accurate. No more than fifty."

City of Crystal Shadow

Seeker stared at Lissyi, speechless and dumbfounded. Finally the Novice found its voice. "Twenty or thirty thousand years from now? The city will last that long?"

"Easily," Lissyi answered smugly. "We Vyinnlyirr build well. As I said, it could even be fifty thousand."

"But . . . but then that couldn't be the reason I was called! I mean, if the danger is still twenty thousand years off, there is no reason to call a Questioner for help . . ."

Lissyi cocked its head to one side as if listening to the ground. "No, that cannot be the reason you were called, Questioner. That is true. You have answered one question truly. But there still remains another and more important one. Why is the city dying? Perhaps that is the question you were called to answer. Why is the city dying?" With that, Lissyi turned and began to stalk away.

"But all things die, Lissyi!" Seeker called out in protest.

Lissyi stopped and half turned back to the Novice. "Oh, yes. But they die in different ways at different times according to their nature. The question about the city of light and air is why it is dying now and why in this way. The answer to that will tell you of its nature. Oh, yes, that is the question!" Lissyi turned away and moved off once more, its stride determined.

Seeker stood deep in thought and watched the blind Vyinnlyirr go.

The Novice walked and walked. It had left the lower level and climbed several levels higher in the city. It was determined to find the sides of the dome and see if it could see out and catch a glimpse of the waste. It didn't know what it expected to see, but it was determined to look.

It walked and walked, taking as direct a route as seemed possible. Since the dome appeared to be a hemisphere, walking straight in any direction should eventually bring the Novice to the dome itself.

It walked and walked. After three feeding periods had elapsed, it realized it was going in circles.

"Why can't I find a way to the sides of the dome, Thryimm?" Seeker asked innocently.

"Why would you want to go to such a place?" Thryimm countered with equal guile.

"Why not? Is it forbidden?"

"Forbidden? No, not forbidden. But not necessary, so no way was provided."

Seeker shook its head. "No, it's more than that. It isn't just that no way was provided. It's that any way was hidden. All the streets, all the bridges, everything is subtly constructed to turn one away, ever so gently, ever so unnoticeably, from the edges of the dome. I know, Thryimm. I've tried every way on every level in this part of the city."

Thryimm gave Seeker a considering glance. "The Questioner is indeed thorough," the Vyinnlyirr said softly. "But the Questioner could have saved a great deal of effort by simply asking."

Seeker gave the Vyinnlyirr equivalent of a sarcastic smile. "That's exactly what I am doing right now. Are you going to give me an answer?"

The Vyinnlyirr sighed deeply. "Imagine, Questioner, living forever in a city you could not get out of, a city surrounded by death and desolation, by a world that was uninhabitable, unlivable. Would not many crave the freedom of the outside? Might they not go to the edge of the city, no matter how vast and wonderful it was, and stare longingly at those wider, forbidden horizons? And what would happen to minds so taken out of their natural environment, their only environment on a hostile planet, taken out and sent on wings of wish far beyond the city?

"At first we had ways that lead to the dome, Questioner, so we found out. Those ways led to madness. The Vyinnlyirr, no less than other sentient species, have spirits that crave freedom. But our destiny is to find our freedom in the Project, to realize our spirit through the Project.

"The outside was a distraction, a danger, an invitation to madness. So we cut it off, turned all ways inward toward the center, in the direction we are destined to follow. Inward back to the city and to ourselves." Thryimm fell silent and stared fixedly at Seeker. "Do you understand, Questioner? Can you understand?"

Seeker stared back, the silence stretching out between the two of them like thin, delicate crystal. Finally Seeker nodded slowly and said, "Perhaps I can. Perhaps. But still I would like to see the outside. I would like to go to the edge of the dome and look out at the waste. Can this be done?"

Thryimm stood so still and silent for so long that Seeker

began to wonder if the Vyinnlyirr had fallen asleep or gone into a coma. Finally Thryimm shook itself as if coming suddenly awake. "Yes," it replied in a softly hissing voice. "Yes, it can be arranged. But we cannot guarantee what will happen to Thassyil's mind. We cannot guarantee the sanity of your host once it sees the outside."

"Do the Vyinnlyirr go insane often?"

The Leader paused in its walking and stroked its beak for a moment before starting off again. "Often? No, not often. There is a certain danger inherent in the Project. Whenever one goes into oneself, that danger exists. Yes, insanity is always possible. But often? No, not often."

"What happens to the insane ones? The rare ones who go insane?" Seeker asked softly.

The Leader shook its head sadly. "They are Released."

"'Released'? What does that mean?"

"Most of them want to leave the city. That is the form their insanity generally takes. They become oppressed by the omnipresence of the city and the ubiquity of the Project. They feel there are eyes everywhere watching them, weighing them, measuring, judging, prying. They want to leave the eyes, the prying behind. They want to leave the city."

"And go where?"

The Leader shrugged. "Nowhere. There is nowhere to go. Oh, most of them want to go home, back to our original home, back to the freedom beneath the double suns, to fly and glide once more in the light. But that is impossible. That world is no more. There is only this world, this city and this waste."

"So they go outside, into the waste?"

After a long pause, the Leader nodded reluctantly. "Yes. They go out into the waste. To die."

"To die," Seeker echoed.

"Yes, to die." The Leader stopped and lifted its arms. "Look at it, Questioner. There it is. We are come by secret ways to the side of the dome almost at ground level. Look and behold the waste. And see why the insane ones go there to die."

As far as the eye could see, the sand and gravel rolled on in shifting hills and valleys. A wind blew and swirled dust devils into the air, dancing them across the hills to die sudden deaths in the valleys. No plant life showed anywhere. The desolation was utter and total.

"There is no surface water anywhere out there," the Leader intoned mechanically as it stood by Seeker's side and stared out at the waste. "A few forms of plant life cling here and there in the bottoms of the deeper valleys. Two or three species of insects feed on them. And there are a few species of lizards and snakes that feed on them and on each other. Aside from that, nothing.

"The temperature is well below freezing during the night and barely climbs higher than freezing in the day. The wind scours the landscape constantly, sucking up life and moisture wherever it might try to collect. The air has barely enough oxygen to support life. And there are other gases, poisonous ones, that rot and corrode the lungs, killing slowly, painfully, but surely."

"How long could one of the Children of Light and Air survive on the surface?" Seeker asked.

"Survive? Not long. Most of those who go out last a few hours. None could last more than a day and a night. There are no food dispensers in the waste, Questioner. No sources of water or nourishment. Even the flesh of the few lizards and serpents is poisonous to our metabolisms. The proteins are all wrong. There is no way to survive out there."

"Then those who go out are going to certain death?"

"Yes. To certain death. There is no freedom beyond this dome, this city. The only freedom is inward, not outward. Outward there is only death and desolation. Hope lies only within the Project. Without lies only despair.

"No Vyinnlyirr is forced to leave the city, Questioner. No force is necessary because there is only one flock here. One flock, with no Leader. I merely hold a meaningless title. I don't really lead anyone or anything. We are one flock, one. Everyone wants the same thing, everyone is the same thing. Whoever feels different . . . well, that one is insane and goes willingly out into the waste. We do not force them. We do not encourage them. They are not one with us. They cannot participate in the Project, and so are of no concern to us." The Leader paused and looked quickly out at the waste that stretched off into the distance. It blinked several times.

"Have you seen enough, Questioner?" the Leader asked

nervously, blinking again. "Are you not ready to go back now?"

Seeker pulled its eyes away from the waste and glanced at the Leader. "Ready to go? No, not quite. I'd like to stay a while longer. I want to walk along the edge here and see the waste from several different perspectives. Do you mind?"

"I . . . I really must be getting back," the Leader said lamely. "Are you sure you are all right? Thassyil is not causing any trouble?"

"No. Thassyil is resting right now, thank you," the Novice said, bobbing its head with respect. "My host will not interfere with my viewing of the waste. But if it bothers you, Leader, feel free to go. I paid careful attention to the route. I'll be able to find my way back when I'm done." And my way back again whenever I want, Seeker added silently.

The Leader nodded several times, shuffled its feet uncertainly, blinked all three eyes, and finally reached a decision. "Yes, yes, then stay by all means. But, ah, I do believe I will be heading back. There is so much to be done on the Project that even a few wasted moments are frustrating. So, then, I'll go. Are you sure you won't come, Questioner?"

"Quite sure," Seeker muttered under its breath as it moved slowly away, the Leader already forgotten, its three eyes scanning the waste for it knew not what.

It took almost four feeding periods to complete the circuit and return to its starting point. The Novice felt weak with hunger and was barely able to restrain the protesting Thassyil. *The body is always harder to control than the mind,* Seeker thought. *I will have to return to the regular part of the city and feed before I lose control of Thassyil's body and mind.*

And what have I learned from my efforts? it asked itself as it stalked back along the hidden ways to the main avenues of the city. *Precious little. The waste appears to be every bit as dead and deadly as the Leader claims. If any Vyinnlyirr, sane or insane, had gone out there, it seemed highly unlikely they had survived much longer than the Leader had indicated.*

Only one trip around, though. Only one circuit. Hardly enough on which to base a final judgment. I must do it again, several times. Slowly, carefully, observing and weighing everything I see. By my pouches, I might be looking at some lifeform and not even realize it! There are plants on my own planet that look for all the world like stones. Why not here as well?

There must be some way to take pellets along so I don't have to come back so often. I'm sure I was so hungry for that last feeding period that I missed a lot. If I fed as I went, I could stay alert all the time. Yes, Seeker decided, I'll have to rig some sort of sack and bring supplies with me.

I wonder if there is any way to get out on the surface itself?

"On the surface itself!?" Thryimm's voice was a startled squawk. "Into the waste? Actually go into the waste?"

"Yes. Actually set foot into it."

"But only the Rejects go..."

"Rejects? Who are the Rejects?"

Thyrimm looked worried. "Um, well, that is what we call those who go insane and have to be, uh, sent out of the city. The Leader mentioned them, yes?"

"Yes. Are there many of them, Thryimm?"

"Oh, no. Only a few every generation. Very few. We are all one flock and..."

"But you do send them out?" Seeker interrupted.

"Unfortunately, yes. We have no choice. We cannot hold them here against their will. They wish to leave the city and the Project and go out. We have no choice but to send them to their deaths in the waste. It is a pity. A terrible waste."

"But they go out. So there must be a way out, Thryimm. Why have I been told before there was no way?"

Thryimm blinked its three eyes rapidly and swallowed several times. "Uh, well, that's not what I meant exactly. I meant there is a way out, but not for normal Vyinnlyirr, you see. Uh, there is no way out because we go inward. So, um," it finished lamely, "I wasn't really lying. You just misunderstood."

"But I don't misunderstand now. There is a way out to the waste. The way the Rejects go. And if I really wanted to, I could go out that same way."

Thryimm nodded reluctantly. "Yes, you could. But I doubt you would live long enough to come back. Thassyil is not a strong Vyinnlyirr mentally. It cannot stand too much stress. I fear going outside would unbalance it. And I understand that if the host goes crazy, then the Questioner..." Thryimm left the thought hanging between them.

"Which may explain why I was given a host with such

beautiful membranes and such a weak mind," Seeker muttered loudly enough for Thryimm to hear. "I am beginning to wonder about a great many things, Thryimm. A great many things.

"I'm not ready yet to go outside, so you can rest your mind on that score for the moment. I need to study the situation more carefully, study the waste from here in the dome. There's no sense going someplace so obviously dangerous unless I'm going for a very definite purpose.

"But that doesn't mean I'll be satisfied with looking at it through the crystal forever. Tell the Leader that, Thryimm. Tell the Leader that I'm going to study the waste as best I can from inside the city but that I may yet want to go out into it."

Thryimm nodded solemnly. "I will inform the Leader of your intention, Questioner." It gave the Novice a short bow and a sour look and left.

Seeker watched it go, a sardonic smile curving its beak. Then it picked up the sack it had filled with pellets and turned the opposite way. Without another look in Thryimm's direction, it set off for the wall of the dome and the view of the deadly surface of the planet.

VII.

Seeker sat down glumly. Nothing. Not a damned thing, it thought disgustedly. It rifled quickly through the pages of the bestiary Thryimm had delivered to its nest. Five species of lizard, two snakes, something halfway between that was especially nasty, twelve types of insects, three arachnids (are they really everywhere in the universe? Seeker wondered), four low bushes, a mosslike grass, several plants that looked like small stones, four that looked like nothing, and one ghastly whatever-it-was that lived buried in the sand and lunged up to grab its prey with pinchers that carried a virulent toxin. And so far as I know, the Novice admitted, I haven't even seen a one of them in five circuits around this damn city. Perhaps the Leader is right. I must be chasing a springdasher. Or a glidewing. There's nothing here. This is a dead end.

But it doesn't feel like a dead end. The Others are more than just a myth or the remnant of a guilty conscience, I'm sure of it. But I've nothing to go on. Just a hunch. With a sigh, Seeker stood and began to walk again, stopping every few yards to gaze out at the waste. Beige gravel stretched out as far as the eye could see. Here and there a dull rock outcropping thrust shattered fingers up out of the gravel. Empty. Desolate. Lifeless.

* * *

It was on the seventh circuit that Seeker suddenly realized it was no longer alone. Another Vyinnlyirr was just visible behind it, walking when the Novice walked, stopping when the Novice stopped, always maintaining the same distance.

Is Thryimm or the Leader having me followed? Seeker wondered. That doesn't make sense. All I'm doing is going around and around in futile circles. Or are they worried I might find something? What should I do now that I've seen my tail?

Seeker sighed and sat down, facing backward along the path it had been following. It made sure the Vyinnlyirr saw it and was aware it had been discovered. For some time, the creature simply stood stock still as if hoping it had not been seen or as if making up its mind whether or not to admit it had been seen. Finally, though, it must have given up or reached a decision, because it began to shuffle toward the Novice. As it came closer, Seeker's sense of excitement began to grow. Unless I'm totally blind, Seeker told itself, that's the very Vyinnlyirr that talked to me in the tower of the Sender and first told me about the Others! It has the same scruffy, disreputable look about it.

As it approached, Seeker sat still and watched closely. I don't want to scare it with any sudden movements, the Novice decided. Slowly, Seeker raised its membranes in greeting.

The strange Vyinnlyirr nodded and failed to respond. "I've nothing much to display in return," it mumbled. "Nothing, no nothing in return. Return. Yes, return is the thing. Return to the air and the breeze."

"You are the one in the tower," Seeker said, trying to control its eagerness.

"Tower, tower, high tower. Yes. The one in the tower. Tower. Spire. Aspire. To greater heights. Sun and light and air and flying softly." It moaned gently, rocking back and forth. "Oh, how this one misses the soft feel of air against its wings."

Seeker cocked its head to one side, confused. "I . . . we talked in the tower of the Sender. You told me of the Others."

The Vyinnlyirr hunched suddenly, fear distorting its features, its two large eyes closed in terror, its third eye blinking rapidly. "Others? Others? There are no Others. Oh, no. A myth, a wish, a hope. But a lie, a lie, a lie! Only one sun now. And no Others. Only emptiness."

It stood upright again and turned its gaze from Seeker to look out into the waste. "And yet," it almost whispered, "and yet, they are there. I see their traces, I hear their soft calling on the wind. 'Come,' they call, 'come to us.' I yearn to go, I yearn."

"Is there . . . is there a way out?" Seeker asked, no longer sure its companion was even cognizant of whom it was talking to. "You hear and see their traces? Where? Show me!"

"See? There, the way the wind swirls that sand? There next to the rock that looks like a finger? There is a print, a track. And there, can you hear the call on the wind? Can you feel them? They are there, just beyond the ridge, waiting."

Seeker stared hard, trying to make out what the other Vyinnlyirr was pointing at. It could see nothing but gravel and rock. No track was visible. The Novice listened with all its might. Could one even hear through this crystal? it wondered. But there was no sound. Not even the wind that listlessly blew the fine gravel up against the crystal could be heard. "I see and hear nothing," it declared flatly.

The Vyinnlyirr cocked its head to one shoulder, a light suddenly going on in its eyes. "Ah," it wheezed. Then it trilled a laugh with a brittle edge to it, one that threatened to shatter and break into despair. "Ah, yes, I know you. You are the Questioner. The Questioner in Thassyil's body. Of course you cannot see or hear. No. Thassyil is blind and deaf and you are doubly so."

"I can see and hear perfectly well," Seeker replied, mildly indignant. "Thassyil is an excellent specimen of Vyinnlyirr."

The stranger laughed fully now, its trill echoing from the hard walls of crystal. "Ah, ah, so you think, so you think! And who told you that, eh? Thryimm? The Leader? Syssyir? The ones, the only ones allowed to talk to you?"

Seeker felt Thassyil shift uncomfortably in its mind. Suddenly the Novice was confused, unsure. What was this creature saying? What did it mean? "Who . . . who are you?"

"I? It doesn't matter . . . ah, but then if it doesn't matter, why not say, eh? Very well. I am Syllini, the Mad One. Mad, they call me," it continued, its voice dropping to a harsh whisper, "ah, ah, mad, yes, but I'm not mad, no, just not like them."

Seeker's confusion grew. "I can see and hear. What are you talking about? You must be mad."

City of Crystal Shadow 67

"Must, must I? Eh, eh? Yes, yes, in a way I am mad. Mad because I am not of the flock. Look at me, Questioner, you can see I am not of the flock. I reject the Project! Reject it! One flock, no leader! Ha! No flock, all slaves!"

"But I'm not blind or deaf!"

"Ha! But you are! They put you in Thassyil, the Sly One, and Thassyil has never given you one bit of help now, has it? Nothing, eh? Eh?"

Seeker felt suddenly cold. "The Sly One? Help? No, no, Thassyil has always been too frightened to help. It . . ."

Syllini's laugh trilled louder than ever. "Too scared? Ah, ah, too scared! Too stupid, yes! Too stubborn, yes! Too obedient to the wishes of the Leader, yes! But too scared? Never!"

"Do you . . . Are you trying to tell me . . ."

"Yes!" Syllini hissed malevolently. "Yes! Thassyil has purposely held you back! Kept you from seeing and hearing things! Ask the Sly One! Ask it, if you dare!"

The Novice had no need to even ask the question. Thassyil was hiding as best it could, radiating fear and guilt. You've . . . you've done these things, Seeker declared silently. Thassyil only whimpered. You will no longer do these things, Seeker ordered, or I will hurt you. By my Nurturer's pouches, I'll thrash you like I would a disobedient cub! Thassyil cringed and shuddered, but agreed. Seeker turned wondering eyes and ears out toward the waste.

"Syllini," the Novice murmured with awe, "I can *see.*"

"Yes, oh, yes," Syllini trilled, "and hear, too!"

"Yes! Yes! And hear, too!" The whistle and hiss of the wind was clear. And on it was borne a high keening call. "That . . . that call," Seeker asked, it's eyes wide with surprise. "Is it always there?"

"Only when they come and hide just beyond the ridge. Only when there is one here, waiting at the edge," Syllini answered, its own face tense with listening. "Only when they know there is one who wants to come out to be with them."

Seeker looked out the sides of its eyes at the other Vyinnlyirr, disturbed by something in the tone of its voice. Syllini was staring fixedly out at the waste, its body rigid. "They are there, beyond the ridge, waiting for me. I must go. They wait. Yes. They. Wait." It began to mutter wildly, its body jerking and twitching. Eyes vague and empty, it began to wander off back the way it had come.

Wondering, upset and confused, Seeker followed, unsure of what to say or do. From time to time, Syllini would suddenly call out as if responding to the call of the wind. Is it really a call, Seeker wondered, or just the noise the wind makes as it slides across the crystal? I see more and hear more than I ever thought possible. I was indeed blind and deaf before. But I still don't see or hear any Others. Or anything else living out there.

Seeker stopped for a moment, a slight movement catching its eye. It turned and stared intently out through the crystal. There, out on the waste, a movement. Was it the wind blowing the fine gravel? Or was it...

Excitedly, the Novice looked up and called out to Syllini. There was no one there! Syllini had disappeared! Seeker ran forward to where it had last seen the strange Vyinnlyirr. Its tracks were there, and they went toward the crystal wall, and...

Stunned, Seeker looked out into the waste. Syllini was there, walking swiftly away from the dome, out into the blowing gravel and sand, out toward the ridge in the distance. Wildly, Seeker searched for the way the Vyinnlyirr had managed to leave the dome. There was nothing there—no door, no window, no hatch, nothing. The crystal was smooth, hard, and flawless. It was impossible to get through it. And yet there Syllini was, striding across the waste toward...

The Novice went rigid. On the ridge toward which Sylini was walking, four figures rose into the wind and light. Heavily cloaked in dull garments that utterly matched the color of the gravel, they rose to full height. Syllini stopped and lifted its tattered membranes in greeting. They raised their cloaks in response.

Then Syllini went to them and disappeared over the ridge in their company.

For a long time, Seeker stood and stared stupidly into the waste. The wind blew the fine gravel into swirls against the crystal. And slowly, softly, the high keening call faded out.

Seeker had never felt so utterly alone in its life.

Both Thryimm and the Leader stood and stared in shock at the Vyinnlyirr that stood defiantly before them. "But... but..." the Leader trilled helplessly.

"I'm going out," Seeker said firmly for the third time.

"Thassyil has agreed to it. Not happily, but agreed. I will protect it and keep it quiescent while we are out there. But I am going."

"There are no Others," the Leader said weakly. "A myth, a wish, a..."

Seeker waved in dismissal. "Don't bother. I've seen them. Not clearly, I grant. They were covered with cloaks, and I have no idea of what they look like. Or even what sort of creature they are." It held up the bestiary. "But I know they're not like anything in here. Syllini went to them and went away with them. I saw it."

"They'll kill the Mad One," Thryimm said grimly.

"Ah," Seeker replied softly, "at last an admission. You do know they are there."

The Leader sighed in defeat. "We know they are there, Questioner. But they are hideous, primitive creatures. Thryimm is right. They will kill Syllini and probably eat it. There is little food in the waste. Syllini would provide several good meals for the whole lot of them."

"They are nomads," Thryimm said. "They live like the vicious animals they are, wandering the waste, eating anything they can get their claws on. Snakes, lizards, carrion, each other, anything. They are vermin."

"If you go out there," the Leader said, taking up the tale, "they will eat you. If you even find them, that is. If one of the snakes or lizards doesn't get you first. Syllini was mad, Questioner, mad. It went out because it was mad. No sane Vyinnlyirr would go out there to die."

Seeker nodded. "But then, I'm not a sane Vyinnlyirr, am I? I'm not a Vyinnlyirr at all. I'm a Questioner. And there's a very big question mark hanging over the waste right there. One I've got to try to answer."

"You will die," Thryimm said flatly.

"That sounds like a threat," Seeker responded calmly.

Thryimm made a disgusted noise and turned away. "You are a fool. You deserve to die. Let it go, Leader. We will be well rid of it."

The Leader looked uncertain. "But suppose..."

"Suppose it comes back? What of it? But it won't come back. Have any of those who have gone out ever come back? You don't have to ask the Keeper of Memories for the answer to that. Let this fool go. We never should have called for a

Questioner in the first place, and so losing one won't matter. We lose Thassyil, of course, but that is no great loss. I will breed again to replace it. Let it go out and be done with this farce."

The Leader gave Seeker a long, cold, considering look. Then finally it nodded. "Very well, Questioner, you will be allowed to go out into the waste. Though we bear no responsibility for this foolish decision. None."

Seeker could hardly hide its smile. "Of course not. I act as all Questioners act—solely on my own authority, which is nonexistent. I go because there is a question that needs to be answered. I don't know if it has anything to do with why you called me, but I think it may. So I go. I will need a few things. Food, weapons, clothes."

"Food we have," Thryimm replied harshly. "Weapons can be made, if you wish. We have no need of them in the city, but there are patterns from the past. Clothes can also be manufactured by the city. Come with me. I will take care of it all and have you on your way as soon as possible."

There was no call on the wind as Seeker stepped out onto the gravel. No line of Others rose from the ridgetop to greet it as it moved away from the side of the crystal dome. The gravel crunched under its feet and the wind whistled softly through its cloak. The pack on its back was heavy, but bearable. Five days food and water. In its left hand was a weapon, a sort of cross between a throwing knife and an axe. Two strangely shaped daggers were in its belt, a sling with a pouch full of smooth pebbles tucked next to them.

Seeker didn't even bother to turn and look behind it as it reached the ridge and gazed out over the vast emptiness of the waste. There is death here, it thought. I may die soon. H*mb*l would dance this desert with grace and ease, but I may die in horror and anguish. Longarm was right. There are an infinite number of ways to die in the universe.

With a short laugh, Seeker strode forward. It hadn't felt this good in years.

In the Waste

Precisely between what is most similar,
illusion lies most beautifully;
for the smallest cleft is the hardest to bridge.

                    Friedrich Nietzsche,
                    Thus Spoke Zarathustra

VIII.

Nothing.

Cold. Wind. Clear, weak sunlight that failed to warm. Sand. Rock. Thin air with a metallic bite that burned the beak and throat. The endless hiss of emptiness. Loneliness so profound the soul feared to gaze into its abyss.

Did I imagine it all? Did I imagine Syllini and those forms that waited on the ridge? Seeker wondered for the hundredth time as it stumbled down a gravelly hill. *I never actually saw any form or even hint of life from the city. Are Thryimm and the Leader right after all? If they are, I'm doomed, for I've gone too far into the waste now ever to return in time. I've walked directly toward the setting sun for five days. My food runs out today, my water tomorrow. If I don't find what I'm looking for, I'll run out two days after that.*

Seeker chuckled grimly. *How bizarre. The bones I'll leave behind won't even be my own!* The Novice pulled its cloak more tightly about its body. *Damn cloak isn't heavy enough for this weather,* Seeker grumbled to itself. *Made for city wear, not for out here in the waste.* *Cold,* it heard Thassyil mumble miserably deep in the mind they shared. *Always so cold.* Seeker nodded stern agreement. *Damn cold, Thassyil. What I wouldn't give for my own natural fur covering right now! Damn Vyinn-*

lyirr fuzz feathers aren't worth a spoiled protoegg. Stupid cloak isn't much better. Your city isn't so damn smart after all. Should have known this cloak wasn't warm enough.

The Novice climbed to the top of the next ridge slowly. Getting weaker, it thought. It coughed, throat raw and lungs irritated by the air. Wonder how long it takes this air to corrode the lungs? Seeker idly asked itself. A lot longer than either Thryimm or the Leader thought. At least there's some consolation in that. I've proved them wrong about one thing.

Will I die of hunger, thirst, exposure, or rotten lungs? it continued questioning itself. Anybody want to take any bets? Personally, I opt for thirst. Though with this scrawny Vyinnlyirr body, hunger might win.

At the top of the ridge Seeker stopped and slowly scanned the area. A little higher than the last ridge. A bit better view. Close to the city, the landscape had been primarily piles of gravel and rock upthrusts. The rock had been rotten and crumbly. The further toward the setting sun Seeker had walked, the finer the gravel had become. Now it was like fine sand. It blew with the wind, swirling high at times, but always on the move. The rocks that pushed their way up out of the sand were harder and sharper, more jagged and dangerous looking. They appeared volcanic in origin, though the Novice was far from being an expert geologist.

Seeker gazed and gazed, looking for movement, life, anything that might provide hope.

Nothing.

Another day of walking through cold and nothing. Food sack empty. A bare splash of water left.

Another day. No water now.

Another day.

Another.

It was worst at night. Then the cold came crashing down like a solid weight. Seeker felt as if it couldn't have stood if it had wanted to. There was nothing but to lie there huddled in its cloak, shivering uncontrollably while the cold pressed down, down, squeezing heat and life from the fragile Vyinnlyirr body.

Even the mind worked more slowly, leaden, heavy with the cold. Nothing like this on Labyrinth, the Novice thought. What would H*mb*l do? Dance? How? Too cold to move. Maybe moving would be best, though? Maybe I should dance?

The very thought of dancing made Seeker chuckle ruefully. What a stupid thing to be thinking of! Dancing! I must be delirious or something. Dancing! Best get a grip on myself, or I'll be trying to fly next.

The Vyinnlyirr flew, long ago. Then they glided, also long ago. Had they ever danced?

Seeker's own race never danced. Ran like the wind, yes. Almost flew when I was a Chaser, Seeker thought, the memory a warm spot in its shivering mind. And as a Catcher, I was the strongest of them all! But we never danced. Never even thought of it.

Why dance? What is it, this dancing? This was the first time it had ever asked itself this question. It was amazed. H*mb*l danced and I simply accepted it as something that was done. I never even thought to ask why. H*mb*l just did it. Thisunit didn't, nor Darkhider, nor Bilrog. Only H*mb*l.

Could I dance? Can you dance if you don't know how to dance or why you're dancing? Why dance? H*mb*l did it to move with the world, to become part of it, to merge with it. Why? What did that mean to the hummer?

Slowly, painfully, the Novice struggled to its feet in the darkness. How do you begin dancing? it wondered. Do you have to hear the music? It listened. There was only the moan of the wind. I must be crazy, it told itself. My mind is slipping. Hunger. Thirst. Cold. Exhaustion. It's getting to me.

Dance? Insane to even think about it. I'm weak and sick and probably dying. Besides, there's only the sound of the wind. Well, then, do what H*mb*l would do—dance to that. Move like the hiss and moan. Slide, turn, slide, dip, slide, turn. Rigid and stiff. Seeker moved awkwardly at first. But as its body began to warm up, it moved more fluidly, more swiftly.

Slide, turn, step, twist. Seeker began to feel the Vyinnlyirr body as it never had before. I've been a stranger in here, it realized, just pulling the strings without ever getting to know what the pulling meant and how it felt. Step, step, turn, twist, twirl, slide, lift the arms, flare the membrane, stoop, twist, hop, flap, fly, swoop, rise, turn, dive, fly.

Seeker could feel Thassyil responding, joining the movement. Flap, turn, leap, glide, roll, twist, rise, dive. No words were exchanged, no thoughts. They simply came together and moved as one. Beat the feet against the sand, rise, flare the membranes, peck and twist, roll in the sky, fly and swoop, soar, leap, run, glide, rise, rise, rise!

Twist! Leap! Twirl! Fly! Soar! Swoop! Flare!

FLARE! SOAR! ROLL! RISE! GLIDE! TWIST! DIVE!

They were lost in the movement, joined and unified, merged not only with each other, but with the wind and the sand, the sky and the hard, bright stars that were their audience. They threw themselves around with utter abandon, flying high above forests of dreams, swooping on prey that died in their claws, seeing the plain rise and rise into the sky, nurturing a cub, wandering lost and dying, fighting, living, merging . . . Lungs pumped, legs thrashed, arms waved, eyes closed in ecstasy, time receded, they danced above and beyond it and the world . . . .

Exhaustion came down like a rock and felled them with one stroke. As the darkness swept up over Seeker, it had time for one last thought: I know why you dance on, H*mb*l.

A thin, miserable light crawled over the top of the ridge and shone weakly in Seeker's eyes. The Novice woke coughing, its throat and lungs more painful than ever. Too much exercise last night, it thought ruefully. Dancing should be done only where the air is sweet and wholesome and when one is rested and fit.

Dancing. Suddenly the whole experience came flooding back to it. What insanity! Dancing in the middle of the night! Weak, cold, thirsty, hungry, and yet wasting energy dancing! And yet . . . and yet Seeker did not feel badly about it.

The Novice checked to see if Thassyil was all right. The Vyinnlyirr was still unconscious. I feel differently toward it now, Seeker realized. I flew with it last night, and it ran the plains with me. Something happened and we became one for a time. The Novice knew it still couldn't trust its host, but at least now it felt a sense of companionship and respect for the Vyinnlyirr. Flying must have been wonderful. Even gliding.

City of Crystal Shadow

How stunted their life is now that they are earthbound!

And for the first time I gained a slight glimmer of what H*mb*1 must experience all the time. Ecstasy, a coming out of the self, a joining with something greater and more powerful. Not pretty or happy. Not ugly or sad. It just WAS. And by embracing it, joining it, I somehow embraced all that it was, pain and joy, horror and hilarity. It was as though for the first time in my life I had uttered a gigantic, earthshaking roar of affirmation to life! A great YES to agony and to ecstasy. And suddenly they had not been so far apart nor contradictory. It confused Seeker and made its head spin with strange ideas. No time for that now, it realized as a spasm of coughing doubled it over. I have other things to think of.

Seeker sighed. Not much time left now. No food. No water. Another two days, maybe three. Real delirium before then. Finally, death. The Jumpship would abort the mission, jettison the body in the stasis tank, and head back to Labyrinth. Longarm would be there when the ship landed, would nod solemnly and then turn away with a snort. Another failure.

It took Seeker three tries to rise to its feet. Then it was doubled over with spasms of coughing for some time. Eventually, the Novice straightened up, turned away from the rising sun, wrapped its cloak more tightly about it and began to trudge wearily forward. No sense waiting for death to come. Might as well go out looking for it. As Longarm would say, that's why I'm here.

It almost didn't see the snake until too late. The thing was much larger than the bestiary had said it was. It struck up from out of the sand, half-buried in ambuscade.

Seeker barely managed to dodge the first strike. The second was met with one of the knives. The third never arrived.

It took several minutes for the snake to stop twitching and thrashing in its death throes. The Novice felt a strange mixture of horror and elation as it watched the monster writhe in pain, the knife piercing its head right through the lower jaw. When it finally lay still, Seeker stood and stared at it in wonder. There are living things out here after all, it told itself. And if there's this one, then why not all the others? Even the Others!

It wracked its memory, trying to recall if the flesh of this serpent was edible or not. Must contain liquid in any case,

Seeker realized. Should I take the chance? Do I really have any choice?

Thassyil became violently ill at the very idea of eating the snake raw and retreated deep within its own mind. Seeker gagged at the strange taste of it, but ate slowly and carefully. Need nourishment, need moisture. The snake must have both. No choice. No choice. But the thing tasted vile nonetheless.

The cramps hit about two hours later. Poison, Seeker thought immediately. Damn thing was poison. Doubled over and vomiting, the Novice was wracked by waves of agony. All over, it thought wearily, almost with relief. Finished. Failure.

It blacked out in the middle of a spasm that threatened to break it in two.

The sun was almost to the horizon when Seeker crawled up out of the blackness. Alive, it marveled feebly. Alive after all. Slowly, afraid it was just a delirium that came at the edge of death, it sat up and looked around. Feel better, stronger, it realized with surprise. My head is clearer than it has been for days.

Seeker stood and stretched. Its stomach ached. Its lungs were raw. But it felt amazingly good. Damn snake wasn't totally poisonous. Just mildly so. Or maybe I'm just not used to it yet. Maybe all those years of eating those manufactured pellets in the city did something to the digestive system which made it hard to eat raw meat.

It stretched again. Alive. It felt good. No food left. Water all gone. No way to go back. But alive and feeling alive. Maybe there was hope after all!

Seeker glanced at the feeble sun. Setting in about an hour. Shall I continue on until then or just stop right here? It looked around. Nothing much special about this place. It just . . .

The Novice froze. Over to the left was a low bush, and next to it lay some of the mosslike ground cover it had seen in the book Thryimm had given it. Life. There was a slight movement. An arachnid! And it was stalking an insect that was on the sand next to the plant! Fascinated, Seeker watched the small drama unfold. The spider was swift, but the tiny insect swifter. Disgusted, the arachnid skittered off in search of other prey.

Damn! I was right! Seeker exulted. There is life here!

City of Crystal Shadow

Snakes, spiders, insects, bushes, grass! The Others must be here somewhere, too. And maybe Syllini with them!

I'll walk until it's dark, Seeker decided.

One of the most dangerous predators in the waste hunted in the dusk. A long, slender lizard, it crept along the sides of the hills, blending in almost perfectly with its surroundings. Slowly, carefully it moved. No sudden motions to draw the eye.

It sought anything. Size didn't matter, only its hunger. Its poison was virulent, incredibly swift in acting, but it attacked the nervous system, paralyzing rather than killing. Its teeth were very sharp, even though its mouth wasn't all that big. It would paralyze its prey and then rip small pieces off, over many days, gradually devouring its still-living meal. The lizard ate carefully, avoiding large veins and arteries and other things that might kill its prey too soon. It wanted to keep its feast alive and fresh as long as possible.

When it sensed the large creature blundering up the hill toward it, it froze in place, even though it knew the thing would pass perhaps ten feet away from where it lay. That didn't matter. It moved slowly. But it could also move with blinding speed for short distances. Say, for twenty feet.

It came at Seeker like a blur in the dusk. The pain as it bit into the Novice's leg was shocking and knocked Seeker down to its knees. The blackness came too swiftly for it to even identify the attacker, though Seeker was sure it wouldn't matter even if it could.

The lizard took a small bite from the leg and chewed happily. Food for several days.

Night fell swiftly now. The world turned black. The wind hissed across the ridge, riffling the edge of the cloak that covered the fallen figure. The stars glittered and the ring that surrounded the planet glowed faintly, a narrow band across the sky.

The lizard took another bite, chewed it thoroughly, swallowed, and then, satisfied for the moment, laid down next to its larder and slept peacefully.

IX.

"Lizbitum?"

"Yuh."

"Killaliz?"

"Gottum. Killum. Bringumbac n eatum."

"Bring*um*bac too?"

"Nuh. I say leavum. Nonufliz. Nonufwater. Toomanyus. Noneedum. Leavum."

"Yuh. I say takum. Gotthisfar. Nodope. Nufliz, nufwater. Usneedum workwork. Takum."

"Ummmm. Isay takum. Frumciti. Smartboy maybe. Can useum workwork. Nufliz, nufwater. If no, eat*um* likeliz. Twothreeday eateat. Takum."

The three heavily cowled and wrapped figures rolled Seeker into a hammocklike net. Two of them grasped opposite ends of the net, hoisted the Novice from the ground and began to carry it off deeper into the waste. The third figure gazed around the area hopefully, as if looking for more of the lizard's paralyzed prey. Then it shrugged, slung the dead lizard over its shoulder and followed the other two.

Seeker's eyes opened.

"Umwakeup," a harsh voice said from left of the Novice's

head. Seeker tried to turn toward the voice. The muscles would not respond. Pain welled up suddenly from the left leg. Seeker groaned.

"Yuh. Umwakeup Umnotmovemove yet. Lizbit twothreedays movemove then. Yuh." This came from a second voice to the right. A vague shape moved into sight. Seeker could make out no face, only a deep cowl fastened so that a small space was open to peer out of. It was too dark for the Novice's gaze to penetrate within. Besides, its eyes weren't working at all well. "I say twothreeday workwork. Maybe smartboy. If not, eatum."

Seeker closed its eyes. Its mind was dull and loggy. Think, it ordered itself, damn you, think! But the task was too difficult and the body overruled the mind. Seeker fell back into unconsciousness again.

The pain brought the Novice back to wakefulness. It was sharp and localized in the right leg. Its eyes opened. There were two shapes, cowled and covered completely as before. One was poking at Seeker's leg, probing the spots that hurt so badly. The other was simply watching.

Seeker groaned. "Umwakeup," the figure poking at its leg said. "Toluso. Pokumleg, wakumup. Now workwork." The two figures grabbed Seeker by the shoulders and lifted it until it was standing. Without another word, they half led, half dragged the Novice through an opening and down a short corridor.

Seeker looked around in astonishment. The chamber it had been in was cut from rock! And so was the corridor. The air was warm and slightly moist. It looked down at its leg, which hurt abominably. Two large wounds gaped there, wounds that were empty holes slightly scabbed over and oozing pus. By my pouches, Seeker thought, what happened to me? Where am I? And what are these creatures carrying me?

Memory came back in a flood. The Crystal City, the waste, the food and water running out, dancing beneath the stars and the light band of the ring, the snake, gorging on its raw flesh, vomiting, bent over in pain, feeling better, and then the sudden flash of life in the dusk, the pain in the leg and the blackness. "What . . . what are you doing?" Seeker muttered in confusion.

The two figures stopped. "Umwalknow. Nocarrycarryum. Umwalknowself," one of the two demanded. The other nodded agreement and the two stepped away from Seeker. The Novice swayed uncertainly for a second, then caught its balance.

It looked inquisitively at the two figures. Both were shorter than Thassyil. That was all the Novice could say for sure. What manner of creature they were was utterly impossible to tell. They wore beige cloaks of some rough fabric that covered them totally, from the cowls that hid their heads to the hem that swept the floor. Only a tiny space was open through which they could look out at the world. But it was impossible to see within. "Who . . . who are you?" Seeker asked shakily. "Where are you taking me?"

One stepped forward and pointed a sleeve at Seeker. "Umworkworknow. Lizbitum, umsick. Nowum nosick, so umworkwork. Headman cumback, talktalk later."

Seeker stared uncomprehendingly. The speech sounded vaguely familiar and meaning was tantalizingly near. But it all seemed as much gibberish as communication. What should I do? The Novice wondered. The second figure gestured peremptorily in the direction they had been walking. "Cumcum. Walkwalk. Workworknow. Talktalklater. Yuh."

Unsure what had been said, Seeker nodded and replied, "Yuh."

The task it was put to was simple. It was handed a small club, flat on two sides, and by gesture and unintelligible words was shown how to swing it against a pile of short stalks that Seeker recognized as one of the plants that was shown in the book Thryimm had given it. The stalks were pounded carefully until they broke apart into separate fibers. Then the two robed figures gathered up the fibers and took them away, bringing back more stalks in their place. One of them always stayed close by Seeker, however. They are my guards, the Novice realized in surprise.

The job was tedious, but not hard. The pain in Seeker's leg and the sudden realization of extreme hunger and thirst, however, made it grueling. The Novice grew weary very swiftly and began to feel faint.

Before long, though, a third figure showed up with what could only be a water bottle and three packets of what Seeker hoped was food. Tiny cups of water were poured from the bottle. It was barely a mouthful, and Seeker foolishly gulped it down in one swallow. Tisking disapprovingly, the two guards

City of Crystal Shadow 83

sipped slowly, savoring the moisture carefully.

Then they opened the packets. Seeker assumed it was food, although the Novice hadn't the slightest idea what it could be. There was a small piece of grey, nasty-tasting, fleshlike material; three black, hard things that might be a kind of flavorless nut; and two dull green, fairly stringy stalks that had a bitter aftertaste.

When the meal was over, Seeker still felt ravenously hungry and thirstier than ever. But the two guards made it quite plain that the work was to recommence. Dully, weak and faint, Seeker grasped the club and began to beat the stalks again. It soon lost track of time, simply beating the stalks, its mind in a haze of pain, hunger, and thirst.

"Stopstop," ordered one of the guards. "Noworkworknow. Nowtalktalk. Headman herenow. Yuh." They gestured to Seeker to follow and set off down another corridor.

After no more than a dozen paces, they entered a larger room. There were perhaps fifteen or twenty cowled figures standing silently around its edges. In its center sat a single figure. A murmur ran around the chamber as Seeker entered behind its two guards. They led their charge up to the lone figure, bowed slightly, and then stepped back two paces.

Observing the obvious formalities, Seeker bowed slightly to the figure and then studied it. There was little to see. Like all the others around the chamber, it was heavily cowled and completely covered up. Not a piece of bare skin, flesh, features, scales, or whatever showed. There was no way of telling what manner of creature lay beneath the robes. It obviously had two arms. But there could be one leg, ten, or none. And the rest of the body, not to mention the head, was an utter mystery.

If these are the Others, then are they the descendants of the original inhabitants of the planet? Seeker wondered. Are these the children of the creatures that refused to enter the city with the Vyinnlyirr, the creatures the Children of Light and Air claim were little better than savage animals? Savage they might well be. But they were hardly animals. They obviously had a language, even if Seeker couldn't understand it. And they lived in a sort of vast cave which they had obviously built themselves in some manner. They wore clothes, had some rudimentary social order, even a technology of sorts. In other words, they were likely sentient. But as Longarm had told Seeker again and again, there was sentiency and there was sentiency. Sentiency made species dangerous as often as it made them reasonable.

The seated figure spoke. "Wherecumfrum? Citi? Yuh?"

Seeker concentrated as hard as it could on the sounds. They sounded vaguely familiar, vaguely like... like...

Degenerate form of our own language, a voice said from within its mind. Thassyil! Seeker replied with relief. I thought something had happened to you. I didn't hear you or even sense you and I thought...

I'm still here, came the reply, wary and unsure. Weak and confused, but here. The creature there, it's talking something like our language. Listen.

"Tellum! Cumcumciti? Yuh?" the seated figure demanded again. An angry murmur was raised around the chamber. Seeker heard murmurs that sounded like "Dumboy" and "Eatum." The Novice concentrated. "Tellum." Tell him? Perhaps, tell me? "Cumcumciti?" Ah, yes, come come city! Do you come from the city? the seated figure was asking! Thassyil agreed silently, disgusted at the primitiveness of the language.

Seeker nodded. "Yes," it replied. "Cumcumciti."

"Ah," the seated figure nodded with relief. A general sigh went up from the chamber. "Smartboy," Seeker heard murmured. "Cumcumciti," the Novice ventured. "Walkwalk eightnineday."

"Yuh," the seated figure agreed. "Tenday. Lizbit, eateat. Killaliz. Bringbringhere. Workworkum."

The Novice felt a sudden surge of exhilaration. I'm talking to them! I'm making myself understood! I've found the Others! "Yuh," Seeker said. "Workworkhard. Umstrong."

"Drinkdrinkfast," said one of the guards from behind Seeker. There was a general ripple of laughter. The Novice felt better than ever. They can laugh! "Thirstythirstythirsty!" Seeker said. There was another slight laugh.

"Alltimeum thirstythirsty. Nonufwater. Nonufliz. Alltime thirsty, alltime hungry," the seated figure replied. Seeker realized that this must be the headman the two guards had said wasn't herenow while it had workworked. "No workwork, eatum. Allsame. No workwork, eatum."

Not enough water, not enough food. Everyone worked or was eaten. It was plain. Seeker understood. It tapped its chest and nodded vigorously. "Workworkum. Workwork yuh!"

"Workworkum alone, yuh? No guards. Guardsworkwork too. No time guard, workwork. Workworkum alone, yuh?"

"Yuh! Workwork!" Seeker mimicked the process of beating the stalks. "Bambam! Workwork!" The laughter was loud this time.

Seeker was fed again and given another cup of water. This time the Novice sipped slowly. The water bearer nodded approvingly and gave Seeker a food packet. Seeker ate mechanically, ignoring the strange, unpleasant tastes. Its stomach felt tight and sore, but not as bad as it had after eating the snake. Adjusting, it thought. Getting used to the food. Learning to speak the language. Soon I'll be a real native.

After working for what seemed like hours, Seeker was finally led to another, tiny chamber. Its guide made it understand it was to rest there, to sleep, or whatever the Others did. Off to one side of the chamber, there was a hole for sanitary purposes. Other than that, the room was bare. Seeker lay down on the stone floor and almost instantly fell into an exhausted sleep.

Seeker worked and ate and slept. Then worked and ate and slept again. There was no daylight, so the Novice had no idea how much time was passing in the outside world. The cave could be near the surface or hundreds of feet below it, for all Seeker knew.

Slowly but surely, Seeker began to regain its strength. The food was scant and the water even more so, but the Vyinnlyirr body began to adapt to the situation. And most remarkably, Seeker noticed, its lungs and throat no longer hurt so badly either. The wounds on its leg healed slowly and painfully, but soon stopped oozing pus and scabbed over thoroughly.

The Others remained as much a mystery as the first time Seeker had seen them. The Novice saw only a few of them, and those not very often. There was one that came and got it every morning and took it to where it worked, then returned it to its sleeping chamber after work was done. Another brought food and water twice a day. And a third came to bring new stalks and take away the beaten fibers.

What in the world are they? Seeker wondered for the hundredth time as it rhythmically beat the stalks with its club. Primitive animals, Thassyil replied. We tried to help them, long, long ago. They refused. You think they are sentient. They are not. Just clever animals.

No, Seeker, responded, you're wrong. They're intelligent. Do you remember what they are supposed to look like?

Thassyil shuddered. Horrible. Scaly. Big lizards. Nasty.

You're just saying that, Seeker scolded. Do you really remember? I never did find any memories of what they looked like when I was with the Keeper in the city. That's odd, too, now that I think about it. I got very clear images of those creatures you fought for supremacy of your original world. Why nothing of these infamous Others?

Thassyil withdrew and fell silent. All right, Seeker said, I won't probe. You Vyinnlyirr certainly have a lot of things you keep secret. You don't make things easy for a Questioner. So you say the Others are big lizards, huh? Could be. The only things that seem to have survived out here in the waste are lizards, snakes, insects and arachnids. They aren't snakes, and I doubt they're insects or arachnids, so maybe they are lizards. But why do they speak a language related to your own, Thassyil? Seeker asked, trying to coax the Vyinnlyirr back into conversation.

They lived with us and worked with us for thousands of years. At least some of them did, the Vyinnlyirr replied. I guess it must have become their language, too. Or at least a degenerate version of it. So we could communicate. How do I know? Ask the Keeper.

Huh, Seeker snorted. Sure. That's a great idea, Thassyil. I'll just trundle on over and ask the Keeper. It's bound to have just the memory I need. Great idea. I wonder which bridge leads there? And Seeker pounded the stalks a little harder in frustration.

Two came for Seeker in the middle of its sleep period. "Cumcum," they said peremptorily. "Now."

They conducted the Novice back into the large chamber where it had first met the headman. Once again, there were cloaked and hooded figures around the edges of the room. This time, however, there were two figures seated in the center. One was undoubtedly the headman. The other one Seeker didn't recognize. It seemed strangely awkward and out of place, slightly taller than the headman and ill at ease.

Seeker bowed to the two of them and the headman bowed

back. "Knowum?" it asked the figure by its side. "Umcumcumciti. Knowum?"

From the depths of the hood, Seeker felt a deep and concentrated gaze. For a long time silence held the chamber in its grasp. Then, slowly, the figure nodded. "Yuh. Knowum."

"Ah," the headman said and nodded. "Good. Knowum. Workworkhard. Noeatum. Umknowum."

The figure next to the headman reached up and pulled back its hood. "Yes," it said distinctly, "I know this one. This is the body and mind of Thassyil, but inside it is another. A Questioner."

The face that emerged from the hood was that of Syllini.

Seeker stared in wonder. "Syllini," it breathed softly. "You made it. You survived."

The Mad One nodded and smiled. "Yes. They came for me and I went to them. They took me in and made me well again. I am Syllini no longer, mad no longer. Now I am Llirr, the Wind Singer, for I sing songs of Wind and Light for the Vyinnlyirr."

"For the Vyinnlyirr?" Seeker asked in astonishment. "Then you've gone back to the city?"

Llirr smiled again. "No, Questioner. I will never go back to the city again. There is only death there. I stay here where there is life. I stay here with the true Vyinnlyirr."

Seeker was stunned. "True Vyinnlyirr? Here? What do you mean? What . . . ?"

The headman put a hand to his hood and pulled it back. A smiling Vyinnlyirr head emerged. One after the other, those standing around the room followed suit until everywhere Seeker looked it saw grinning Vyinnlyirr faces.

"The true Vyinnlyirr are here, Questioner," Llirr said softly.

Deep in its mind, Seeker heard Thassyil scream.

X.

"These tunnels and caves," Llirr explained as it walked with Seeker and the headman through the corridors of the Vyinnlyirr nest, "are left over from the mining that went on thousands of years ago when the Children of Light and Air built the city. The whole planet is honeycombed with them, for every last ounce of useful material was ripped from the earth. Now," it said, making a sweeping gesture with its arms, "all that is left is the bare rock itself. No metals, nothing. Everything of value was taken for the city."

"Are there many of them inhabited like this one?" Seeker asked. "Are there Vyinnlyirr living in caves all through the waste?"

Llirr smiled sadly. "No. There are many tunnels, of course. But most have collapsed during the thousands of years since they were built. And many were not habitable in the first place. But more important is the simple fact that the Vyinnlyirr of the waste are few in number. Very few."

"Notnufliz, notnufwater," the headman said grimly. "Hardlive. Manydiedie. Lizkilum. Snakekilum. Yuh."

"But the waste is vast," Seeker protested. "The city covers only a tiny percentage of the planet. The rest is the waste. Surely there are many more Vyinnlyirr here than in the city."

Llirr shook its head and sighed. "No. Most of the waste is truly empty. It is only here, near the city, that the caves and tunnels have inhabitants.

"You see, Questioner," the Vyinnlyirr continued, "these people are all descended from those who, like me, could not stand living in the city and escaped to the waste. Many died before they could find shelter and food. Many failed to adapt. It must have been especially hard for the first ones. They were very brave. Now at least there are Vyinnlyirr already here, already established.

"But though we have extended our range many days away from the city, we are still inhabiting only a small ring of the waste that surrounds the city. About how far out are there Vyinnlyirr, headman?" Llirr asked.

The headman thought for several moments. " Ummmmm. Maybe fivedaywalk more. Maybe sixsevenday. Notenday. Nuh."

Llirr nodded. "That's what I'd heard. About twenty days of walking from the city everything ends. No more Vyinnlyirr."

"How many of you are there, then?"

"Oh, I imagine some thirty to fifty thousand."

"And of course, even though they denied it to me, the Vyinnlyirr in the city know you exist?"

Llirr thoughtfully cocked its head to one side. " Hmmmmm. I think they know, deep down, that those who leave the city survive. But they don't like to face up to the idea. It rather contradicts everything they believe in. After all, if there are Vyinnlyirr living here in the waste, what does that mean for the Project? The point of the Project is to find out everything about the Children of Light and Air. If there are Vyinnlyirr out here that they don't know about, then the Project is doomed to failure, isn't it?"

"The obvious solution would be to either exterminate you or force you back into the city," Seeker suggested.

Llirr nodded. "Obvious, yes. But more easily said than done. There was a time, many thousands of years ago, when they did try halfheartedly to capture or wipe out the people of the waste. The problem is that no maps exist of all these tunnels. So the searching had to be on foot. It was dangerous, grueling work and the city had no real heart for it. The Project absorbs all the energy and time they have. Now the entrances to the tunnels are well camouflaged against the possible recurrence of just such an attempt. I doubt they will try again. It's simply easier to deny there are any Vyinnlyirr out here than it is to seek them out and destroy them."

They walked in silence for a moment. Then Llirr said softly, "But the real question is what is to be done with you."

Seeker stared at Llirr in surprise. "Me? What do you mean?"

"Well, you obviously didn't come here to join the people of the waste. You're a Questioner, and so I assume you came here to learn something. But, you see, *we* didn't call you. What is it you want? The headman and all the rest are quite concerned about what you intend. As you can imagine, they're a bit suspicious of anything that has to do with the city. And you came out without being called, on your own, no one expecting or waiting for you."

"They were waiting for you?"

Llirr nodded. "Yes, of course. They had come for me, for they sensed my distress and came. It was their calling that I heard and that led me to the edge of the dome. Don't you remember? Or didn't you hear it?"

"I thought I heard something, once Thassyil allowed me to hear properly. But I wasn't sure what it was. A kind of high keening sound that could just as well have been the wind."

"It wasn't the wind. But that doesn't answer my question. What are your intentions, Questioner?"

The Novice thought for a few moments and then replied carefully. "I really don't have any intentions. Other, that is, than learning what I can about the people of the waste.

"You see, Llirr, I still don't know why I was called down to the planet by the Vyinnlyirr. The Leader won't give me any direct answer when I ask it. Nor will Thryimm or anyone else. So I really don't know what I'm looking for. Perhaps if I gather enough information, some kind of pattern will emerge. Perhaps not. I just don't know."

"But you do intend to return to the city, don't you?"

"Yes, eventually I must."

"That's the problem. The headman and the others are worried you might give information on the location of their nest to those in the city. They fear the possible repercussions of the Vyinnlyirr in the city finding out for sure that they exist and where to find them."

"But you yourself said they haven't made any attempt to

harm the people of the waste in thousands of years," Seeker protested.

Llirr shrugged. "Because they've half-managed to convince themselves the Others are just a myth. I'm not sure what would happen if they knew the myth was reality. And that the reality was that Vyinnlyirr can and do survive in the waste." Llirr turned and stared intently into the Novice's eyes. "You must have realized by now that they are insane, Questioner. The whole city, the whole race, utterly mad! The Project, the Project! That's what has driven them into the abyss. They raped and destroyed a whole world just to build that city so they could work on the Project. And they have locked themselves away from life for so long that they no longer understand it.

"Look around you, Questioner. What do you see? You see Vyinnlyirr, true Vyinnlyirr, creatures who work and laugh and sing and love life. Did you see anything this healthy, this sane, anywhere in the city? Did you hear laughter? Did you hear singing? Did you even sense happiness?

"Oh, yes, the people of the waste live a very hard existence. Much harder than those in the city who have everything provided for them. Here they die very real and very painful deaths. That lizard that bit you would have eaten you alive, slowly. And there are serpents here whose bite leaves one to die hideously, covered with ghastly lesions and arching in the agony of convulsions that snap bones like sticks. Hunger kills, and thirst.

"But there is life here! Life!" Llirr stopped suddenly. "Ah, but those are just words to you now. You have seen almost nothing yet. When you live among these people for a while, you too will become sane. Perhaps even Thassyil will become sane. If you are allowed to live among them, that is."

Seeker caught the hint. "What do you mean, 'if'?"

Llirr sighed. "This long tunnel goes on for miles. We are going with the headman to another nest. There we will sit in council with the headmen from all the nests in this immediate area. They will decide what to do with you."

"What are the possibilities?"

"Well," Llirr replied, "there are several. First, they may simply decide to kill you and eat you. They're always short of food. Second, they may send you back out into the waste to die. Exile you, so to speak. Third, they may keep you in the nest, working, for the rest of your life. Fourth, they may adopt you into the flock as they did me. Fifth, they may give you some kind of special status, since you are a Questioner, and allow you to come and go as you please. That's what I've suggested to them."

Llirr stopped and looked appraisingly at Seeker. "There's only one problem with that, Thassyil. You're in Thassyil's mind, and anything you experience, Thassyil has access to. That worries me and the people of the waste. I think they would be willing to trust you, Questioner. But they worry about Thassyil and what it will do once you are gone."

The Novice was thoughtful. "I don't know the answer to that, Llirr. Thassyil is . . . hiding right now. I can't even sense it, though I know it's there somewhere. The shock of finding out that the Others were actually Vyinnlyirr was too much, and Thassyil has gone into hiding. Perhaps when it comes out again I will be able to talk with it. We have become much closer as a result of the experiences we had in the waste. Perhaps . . ."

"Perhaps," Llirr said, "will not be enough for the people of the waste. I don't know what will be enough. But we can only hope for the best. Let us concentrate on walking now. We have a long way yet to go."

The chamber they finally entered was the largest Seeker had seen so far. It was at least twenty feet by thirty, and the ceiling rose more than twenty feet overhead. A small crowd awaited them.

The headmen sat in a circle and got down to business quickly. The one from Seeker's nest rose and said, "Wefindum lizbit. Bringbringnest. Workworkgood. Yuh."

"Cumcumciti, yuh?" one of them asked.

"Yuh, cumcumciti," Seeker's headman replied. "Smartboy. Workworkgood."

"Notnufliz, notnufwater," one dour individual said. "I say kilkil, eateat."

"Nuh," yet another replied. "Smartboy workwork. Not eateat. Um goodgood. Keepum. Yuh."

It went around from one to the other for some time, each expressing his opinion and then changing it. Seeker was not sure who was against it and who for. Finally Llirr stood and spoke at length, telling them who and what Seeker really was, a Questioner that had come from afar, called by the Vyinnlyirr of the city. This revelation prompted another round of questions and opinions, and once more Seeker was not too sure who was for and who against.

The process went on and on. Food and water was served to all and the discussion continued. Everyone spoke several times on every issue. Seeker tried the best it could to follow what was said, but the dialect was still strange and hard to understand.

Eventually, though, the whole thing ground to a halt. All eyes turned to Llirr. The Vyinnlyirr looked at Seeker, nodded slightly, and stood. It stepped out into the center of the circle, took a deep breath, and began to sing.

Seeker was surprised. It had never heard any of the Vyinnlyirr sing before. Llirr's voice was high and thin, but very clear and beautiful. The words were strange at first, but the Novice soon realized they were from a far more ancient form of the Vyinnlyirr language.

> "Soaring cloudlike, into air,
>   Light calls you, calls you,
>   Wind is crying, wailing like a child,
>   Lost, alone, flying high, away,
>   Whirling skyward, wraith of airlight..."

The song was sad and filled with a vague longing that made Seeker's throat swell. Before the Novice realized it, it was standing and swaying to the rhythms. The others were also on their feet.

Slowly they all began to move, shifting their weight from one foot to the other, lifting their arms, turning, bending. Gradually they picked up momentum and speed.

The song led them, set their pace.

> "Stooping now, swooping now,
>   Prey is running, fleeing, hiding,
>   Talons strike, red blood flowing,
>   Flowing screams of pain and anguish,
>   Ripping beak, bloody slasher..."

They dove and swooped, twirled and leapt, their robes flaring out around them. Eyes glazed, beaks hung open, tongues lolled out. They threw themselves about, Seeker with them, in their midst, dancing, merging, forgetting, remembering. The song rose and soared with them, keeping pace, driving them on to new heights, flying next to them as part of the flock. They fell back into time, back into a more primitive state of their minds, deep down beneath the layers of civilization. There, in passion, pain, and joy, they reveled and danced, blended, individuation gone.

Eventually, though, the music flagged and faltered. They became tired and their movements slowed. The existence of their race had been long and exhausting. They were climbing back up, or down, from the vigor of its youth toward its end, its today. The bone weariness of their race, the hard life of the waste came back to them once more.

But for a few moments they had escaped. They had joined in one great assent to life, to its pain, to its joy, the two sides of the same thing had merged in them as one whole. And life, even its horror, had been indescribably wonderful and worthy.

One by one, they collapsed. Llirr stopped singing and stood as if stupefied. Eventually, Llirr moved painfully to Seeker's side. The Novice was sitting up, staring around as if suddenly awakened from a deep slumber.

"Come," Llirr said hoarsely. "The decision has been made. We must go now and let them sleep. We need sleep, too. When they awake, they will call for us and you will know your fate."

Someone shook Seeker awake. The Novice had no idea how long it had slept. It felt hungry, thirsty, and disoriented. "Comecome," the Vyinnlyirr that had shaken it said. "Headmen wakenow, talktalk."

The Novice rose groggily and stumbled after its guide. It was only a short distance to the large chamber where the council and the dance had taken place . . . When? Yesterday? A few hours ago? Seeker had completely lost track of time.

The headmen and Llirr had already arrived and were seated. As Seeker was led to its place, it tried to read their expressions for some hint of what had been decided. This is life-or-death, the Novice realized suddenly. The success or failure of my whole mission depends on what these headmen have decided.

Llirr rose and looked over the assembly. "The headmen have asked me to tell you of their decision. They say this is fitting since we both came from the city." There were murmurs of "yuh, yuh," from around the circle.

"Many wished to eat you. But they realized that you have

a special status as a Questioner, even though they did not send for you, and hence as a guest. They will not eat you.

"But though you are a Questioner, you are in the body of a Vyinnlyirr, and one from the city, one who did not come here to the waste of its own accord. So you are also not a guest.

"The Vyinnlyirr whose mind you share is not trusted by the headmen. They know you bear them no ill will. You danced with them as one of them, and this has shown you to be a good creature, whatever your original form. But Thassyil is not trusted.

"So they have decided that you may live among them as a guest. You must work to help pay for your keep. But you may move freely among them. This is the way it should be for a Questioner.

"But you may never go back to the city. The Vyinnlyirr who shares your mind is a potential enemy and might reveal their existence and whereabouts to those in the city.

"You may live. But you may never go back."

Seeker sat quietly, stunned by the decision. Never go back? Then there was no way to complete its mission! It would simply live here in the waste until Thassyil died and then die with it!

But I won't be killed right away, the Novice reminded itself. There is hope as long as there is life. I must keep hold of that idea. There is hope as long as there is life.

Thassyil could be heard dismally wailing deep in its mind. Seeker felt like joining in.

XI.

Seeker was moved from task to task. For several days, its job was to deliver food to those working throughout the tunnels. Then it was assigned to the digging and clearing of one of the corridors. Next it helped to prepare and pack food, cutting up lizards and snakes the hunters had brought in and making up individual servings of the roots, leaves, seeds, and other items those who scoured the waste for edibles managed to find. Then there was the thick gruel that was produced in large pots into which all manner of things were thrown. Seeker never tried to find out what went into the gruel. The taste was foul enough to make such an enquiry counterproductive. Best just to eat the stuff and remain ignorant, the Novice decided.

Between tasks, Seeker discovered it was indeed free to wander about the tunnels and chambers and observe the Vyinnlyirr of the waste. They seemed to be a surprisingly happy lot of creatures, given the grim and grinding nature of their existence. Always on the edge of starvation and death by thirst, they managed to hang on with determination and a sense of humor. The Novice often came upon small groups that had gathered to sing or dance.

Eventually, Seeker asked if it could join the hunting and gathering parties that went every day into the waste in the

City of Crystal Shadow

endless search for sustenance. The headman thought about the request for several days and then gave its permission. Seeker would be allowed to join one of the parties going out to gather plants.

The Novice felt a strange sense of excitement and exhilaration as it stepped once more onto the surface of the waste. It was in the company of four other Vyinnlyirr, all carefully and completely wrapped against the cold. As a body, they moved off in the direction away from the sun that was still just barely above the horizon. Further into the waste, Seeker realized. Perhaps they don't trust me enough to take me in the other direction.

For several hours, the group trudged wordlessly toward the west, Seeker squarely in the middle of the line. They were in an area where there was little sign of life.

At one point, the leader of the group stopped and pointed off their path to the right. The others twittered excitedly. The leader came back to Seeker and pointed again. "Seeseeum that?" it asked.

Seeker stared in the direction the creature was pointing. There was a fairly flat expanse of sand, slowly rising to a ridge in the distance. Two small bushes stood close to each other in the middle of the flat area. Other than the fact that Seeker couldn't remember ever having seen bushes like them before, it noticed nothing else unusual. "I see nothing but two bushes," the Novice told the leader.

The whole group trilled laughter. "Ah," the leader said, "luckyluckyum got walkwalk sofar! Watch!" It looked around briefly until it found a fist-sized rock. Then it gestured toward the two bushes. "Foodfood, eateat by bushes, eh? Maybeyes, maybeno, eh? Walkwalk over findout, eh?" It heaved the rock through the air to land squarely between the two bushes.

The result was astonishing. The ground around the bushes literally erupted. The bushes were attached to something which was hiding below the surface. A mouth, eyes, teeth, and several arms appeared from the sand and grabbed the rock, pulling it instantly out of sight. There was nothing now but a smooth expanse of sand. In a few moments, the bushes pushed back above ground and all was as it had been.

Shaken, Seeker turned to the leader of the group. "What was that?"

The Vyinnlyirr chuckled and the others joined in. "That

badbad, eateat. Nogood food. Kilkilum," it pointed to Seeker, "Kilkil n eateatum. No findum food near bushes likeum, eh? Only diedie near bushes likeum. Stay away, eh?"

The Novice swallowed and looked nervously at the bushes, trying to remember every detail of their appearance. "Yeh," it mumbled, "Yeh, I'll stay far away from any bushes like that."

By the time the sun was setting, they had all returned. Their total take for the day was two bags barely full of nuts and roots. Both bags were emptied into the gruel pots, since the leader had declared none of it fit to eat by itself.

Llirr was waiting with the headman when Seeker returned to the main chamber. "Ah, Questioner," the Vyinnlyirr greeted the Novice, "I understand you were on the surface today? Was it interesting?"

"Very," Seeker replied drily. "Hard work, little return, danger, cold, exhaustion from a long, long walk. How can these people be so cheerful all the time, Llirr?"

Llirr shrugged. "They are free. Not from the necessity of life; no one is free from that. But free from any external restraints they don't impose themselves."

"Free." Seeker mulled that over. "Seems I've heard that before. From the Leader in the city. It claimed the Vyinnlyirr in the city were free because they could spend all their time working on the Project."

The Vyinnlyirr shuddered. "That is not my idea of freedom. I remember it only too well. I've been cured of my madness here in the waste by the true Vyinnlyirr, but I can still remember what it was like to be mad."

"I've been wanting to ask you about that," Seeker said. "I remember you very well as Syllini, and I don't mind saying that the change is dramatic. And so sudden. I mean, it couldn't have been much more than thirty days from the time I saw you leave the city to the time I saw you here. How did they manage to cure you that swiftly? You were in pretty bad shape when I saw you."

The Vyinnlyirr smiled. "They have ways. They are used to it, you know. All those who finally come out of the city are in pretty bad shape. All have to be cured."

"Are they always as successful as they were with you?"

"No," Llirr replied sadly. "Often they come too late and

the poor creature they take from the city is hopelessly insane."

"Too bad," Seeker commiserated. "But that reminds me of something else I was wondering about. How did they know you wanted to leave? You said something about them calling you. How did they know to come and call? Are they there near the city all the time, just waiting and calling?"

Llirr cocked its head to one side and watched Seeker silently for a few seconds. "Ummmmm," it said finally, "I really don't know how to explain it. They just seem to know. They come when someone is ready to come out and call to them. They wait until that one comes out. Then they take it away."

"Hmmmm," Seeker mused. "Strange indeed. Over all that distance, to be able to tell someone is going insane in the city. But I don't understand how, if they come fairly regularly, that no one in the city is aware of their existence. I mean, surely someone must have noticed them."

"Not necessarily," Llirr answered. "Don't forget, the city Vyinnlyirr don't believe in the Others, so they have no reason to look for them."

"Oh," Seeker said, " they believe in the Others, but not in these Others. The Others they talked about were the survivors of the original semisentient species on this planet, the species they claim became extinct as a result of the building of the city. Was there any original species like that, Llirr?"

Llirr shrugged. "I don't know. I've never heard of anything like that being out here in the waste. Perhaps at one time, long and long ago. But now there're only the snakes and lizards. And, of course, the Vyinnlyirr."

"And there's no chance of the Others having survived?"

"How could they?"

"The Vyinnlyirr have managed, and they aren't even native to the planet."

"But we have many advantages the original species would not have had, if they existed. We have our sentience and the network of tunnels. We are a truly intelligent species, Questioner, one capable of building the city. Surely we would also be capable of surviving in the waste if we can do something that wonderful!"

Seeker shrugged. "The one doesn't imply the other. But, no matter. Still, I wonder if there really are Others? After all, I hardly expected to find Vyinnlyirr in the waste. And if I found them, perhaps I might find more."

"But where? Where would they be, Questioner? We Vyinnlyirr roam the whole area and have never found a thing."

"Perhaps further out. I don't know."

Llirr smiled smugly. "I can assure you there is nothing further out. You might as well look for the Others in the city itself as out here in the waste!"

Seeker smiled vaguely and nodded. "You're probably right. Still, I can't help but wonder. After all, I guess that's what being a Questioner is all about."

The Vyinnlyirr leaned slightly forward. "Did you ever figure out why you were called to the city, Questioner?"

The Novice laughed nonchalantly. "No. I could never get a straight answer from either the Leader or from Thryimm. Thassyil doesn't seem to have the vaguest idea. Syssyir had no notion. Even Lissyi could give no answers. I guess I'll never know."

Llirr nodded and smiled with ill-concealed relief. "I suppose not. There are many things which are probably unknowable. But life here in the waste is good. Best just to relax and enjoy it, eh?"

Seeker laughed. "Yes. Especially since I seem to have no choice in the matter!" Nodding pleasantly to Llirr and the headman, the Novice left the chamber.

Once into the corridor and out of sight, it stopped and looked back, a deeply thoughtful frown on its face. Now what was that all about? Seeker wondered. Why is Llirr so anxious about the possibility of Others? Why the evasion as to how the Vyinnlyirr knew it wanted to come out of the city? And why the interest in whether or not I had figured out the reason for the Call?

Something didn't feel right about all this. As Seeker walked slowly back to its chamber it wondered what it was.

Time passed and Seeker learned more and more about the Vyinnlyirr of the waste. And the more it learned, the more suspicious it became. The Novice had gone on many hunting and gathering expeditions and never once had the take been large enough to feed the group hunting, much less all those left behind working. Quite simply, there didn't seem to be enough food to go around, and yet there always was. Despite what Llirr and the headman had said, no one seemed to be starving or dying of thirst.

And that was a second mystery. Where did the water come from? Although invited along on hunting and gathering expeditions, Seeker was never allowed to collect or carry water. Llirr explained, when questioned about it, that the act was sacred among the Vyinnlyirr of the waste and, as an outlander, the Questioner could not participate. The answer was a patent lie and Seeker knew it.

It slowly dawned on Seeker that life among the Vyinnlyirr of the waste was too idyllic, too perfect. They were simple people, on the edge of destruction at all times, yet laughing and happy in their precarious existence. It was almost a stereotype. The noble savage. It just didn't ring true. There were never any fights, never any disagreements, never any frictions between them. They were just too good to be true.

Llirr, the Novice soon realized, was no better about answering questions than Thryimm and the Leader had been. And Seeker got the growing conviction that the Vyinnlyirr's frequent visits were less out of friendship and concern than out of a desire to keep tabs on the activities of the Questioner.

Something was wrong. What?

"This is a good time, Questioner. No one is dying of hunger and thirst because the springs deep in the tunnels are flowing and food is plentiful. Be glad you are here in such a good time. In bad times, you would have been eaten."

"If things are usually so desperate here, Llirr, why do they come to the city for those who want to leave? After all, unless they use them for food, they would just add another mouth to feed."

Llirr trilled nervous laughter. "No, they don't eat those who come out of the city. Those who come out work and pay their own way. Once they are sane again, that is."

"Work? What work compensates for an extra mouth? It couldn't be hunting and gathering. If food is already in short supply, one more hunter would probably not produce as much as it would consume. And only so much water can be carried. How many hoods have to be made, and how often replaced? How many new tunnels need to be cleared? I don't see how it works out."

"It is the sacred obligation of the Vyinnlyirr of the waste to take those from the city that want to leave," Llirr intoned solemnly.

"That seems a strange answer," Seeker replied. "'Sacred obligation'? I've never heard that phrase used before. What does the sacred refer to? Have you deities?"

Llirr became confused. "Sacred means just . . . that we owe it to our race, you see. Yes, that's it. It's part of our racial instinct."

"But not part of the racial instinct of the Vyinnlyirr in the city? Surely they could cure mad ones? Why must they be rescued and cured by those in the waste?"

"The Vyinnlyirr in the city are totally dedicated to the Project. Anyone not serving the Project is considered not worth bothering with. They have lost their racial instinct in the city. They live only to serve the Project, not the race."

"And yet the racial instinct comes back to one when one leaves the city. After all, everyone out here in the waste either is from the city or descended from those who are. Isn't that correct? Very strange."

"There are some questions," Llirr said stiffly, "that are not worth seeking answers for. Instead, why don't you ask about the life of the Vyinnlyirr here in the waste?"

"Llirr, I'm *living* the life of the Vyinnlyirr of the waste. I don't really need to *ask* about it. Just when something seems strange to me. Then I ask." But never seem to get any answers, Seeker said silently to itself.

Llirr stared at Seeker for several long moments, its eyes unusually hard and unfriendly. "Yes," it finally said, "yes, that's true. You are living the life of the Vyinnlyirr of the waste. The hard, dangerous life of the Vyinnlyirr of the waste."

Llirr's slight emphasis on the word "dangerous" brought a chill of premonition to the Novice.

The hunting party went further toward the setting sun than Seeker had yet been. They had set out early in the morning, each carrying a large water bottle and an unusually large food packet. The Novice had inquired if they were going to be out for more than one day. The question seemed to confuse the group leader, and the answer Seeker got was unintelligible.

In fact, as dusk gathered, the party stopped in the lee of a sharp ridge and the leader gave orders to make a camp there. This was a new experience for Seeker. It had never been with the Vyinnlyirr on the surface at night.

Most of the Vyinnlyirr ate almost their entire food packet

City of Crystal Shadow

and drank most of their water. Seeker, feeling very uneasy over the strange situation, ate and drank sparingly. When they had finished, night had fallen and all, after singing a gentle song together, rolled up tightly in their robes and went to sleep.

Seeker mimicked their actions. But it stayed awake and loosened the two knives it carried in its belt.

There were no clouds and the stars shone coldly overhead. The dim glow that marked the planet's meager ring stood directly above. For hours Seeker watched the stars make their way across the sky and studied the ring, wondering idly where its ship was located.

Halfway through the night, the Novice became suddenly aware that two of the Vyinnlyirr were no longer in their original places. It carefully gazed around, trying to move as little as possible, in an attempt to locate the missing ones.

There! Over to the left. They were kneeling together as if conferring. Now they rose and, bent over, cautiously moved in Seeker's direction. As they came close, almost within reach, Seeker caught the slight glint of starlight off something that one of them held in its hand.

Springing suddenly to its feet, Seeker struck out at the two of them with its knives. They squawked and fell back in astonishment. Seeker knew it had hit neither of the two and that they were merely startled. There was no time to waste. Stooping, the Novice grabbed its water bottle and food packet and leapt away, bent and running. As it passed one of the sleeping Vyinnlyirr it grabbed another food packet and water bottle.

The two behind it raised a cry. Others began to sit up in sudden confusion. One tried to grab Seeker, but the Novice slashed downward with a knife and the Vyinnlyirr fell back with a scream, holding its bleeding hand.

A few more steps and Seeker was over the crest of the ridge and down the other side. It ran as hard as it could now, flat out in the direction in which the sun had set. Behind, it could hear the sounds of pursuit being organized.

I've got a good lead, it told itself as it ran. A good lead and a good chance to outrun them. That is, if I don't step on a serpent or lizard or run into one of the things that hides beneath the surface.

* * *

Seeker ran hard for many minutes, then slowed. It stopped and listened. The sound of the chase had died. No one was after it any longer. Had they given up? Or did they just assume that there was no longer any reason to continue the hunt?

After all, the quarry was a long, long way from the city, with limited water and little food. It probably couldn't find its way back to the tunnels it had been living in, and other tunnels were carefully hidden.

Why waste the energy to chase a quarry that was doomed to die in the waste anyway?

XII.

"See anything that looks familiar, Thassyil?" Seeker asked aloud. It wasn't necessary to speak aloud to the Vyinnlyirr whose mind it shared, but the Novice felt an urgent need to hear a voice, any voice, in the midst of the desolate waste.

"Why ask me that?" Thassyil responded querulously. "You know I've never been out of the city in my life. How would I recognize anything way out here?"

"Huh," Seeker grunted noncommittally. "Just checking. One never knows who knows what around this place." The Novice paused as it reached the top of a ridge and looked off eastward. "As I figure it, we're at least eight days walking from the city, maybe ten. We should be able to see it from a day, maybe two, away. It's pretty tall and there isn't much out here to cut the view. We headed due west coming out, so we go back due east. If we are no more than a day off either north or south, we should be able to find it."

"How many more days of food and water do we have?"

Seeker shook the water bottle. "Ummmmm. Maybe two, three. Four if we're really careful. Food should last three days on really tight rations."

"We'll never make it," Thassyil said bitterly. "We're doomed."

"Well," the Novice replied, "I'll admit things don't look too good, but I've been in worse shape in my life. So far, this planet isn't really any worse than Labyrinth. At least the natural part of it isn't. The sentient portion is something else again."

Seeker started to walk. "You know, Thassyil, you've got nothing to lose now by telling me everything you know. I mean, if we're going to die, you might as well make a clean breast of it."

Thassyil was silent for such a long time that the Novice decided the Vyinnlyirr either hadn't heard or had retreated once more into its private corner of the mind they shared. It was a surprise when Thassyil began speaking. "I don't really know that much, Questioner. All of us who work on the Project only work on a tiny little part of the whole. My speciality was the early years of our occupation of the city. I examined mental states resulting from the enclosure and loss of a natural environment. Especially how it affected our sense of time and space.

"When it was decided to send out a Call for a Questioner, I had nothing to do with that decision, by the way, but I was chosen for the task of host. A lot of what I knew was... suppressed, I guess you'd have to call it."

"Suppressed? What do you mean?"

"Well," Thassyil continued, "it's hard to explain, and I don't really know anything about how it was done. It's just that there are certain things I can't even think about any more. I mean, when I do, it either hurts or my mind just slips away from it."

Seeker walked along silently for several moments. "Interesting. You can't push past the blocks? No, I guess not. Hmmmm. You know, Thassyil, there may be another way. Let me pose a problem to you. Call it an approach.

"Let us suppose there was a territory you wanted to know about very badly, say, oh, a section of the city. And suppose further that you weren't allowed to enter that territory in any way. How could you still find out things about that territory?"

Thassyil thought for a few moments. "Well, I could ask Vyinnlyirr who'd been there. Or look up any references to it from past travelers who might have passed through it."

"Good. That's certainly one way. Another would be to circle the territory again and again, noting its size and shape, trying to snatch distant glimpses, things like that. Putting all that together, you could probably develop a pretty good picture of what the territory was like, couldn't you?"

"Probably. Not as good as you could by going there, but probably fairly accurate. What's the point?"

"Well, we have several unknown territories here and I think they overlap. First of all is the question of why the Call was made at all. I can't get anybody to give me an answer to that. Every time I ask, I get the runaround. They change the topic or simply act as if they hadn't heard.

"Second is the question of why parts of your mind were blocked. It seems likely to me that at least one of the reasons the blocks were set up was to make inaccessible precisely the material I might need to figure out why the Call was made.

"Third, there's this whole setup here in the waste with these escaped Vyinnlyirr. There's something wrong about it all, and I suspect it's tied in with the first and the second questions. All aspects of the same central mystery, if you get what I'm driving at. Somehow, it all fits together."

"Possibly," Thassyil said cautiously. "But what has that to do with my blocks?"

"Well, if we walk around the closed-off places in your mind, we might get hints about what is closed off. By seeing what isn't closed off, we might get a fix on what is."

"It might work. I'm willing to try it."

"Good," Seeker said. "I'll ask questions and you try to answer them. When we come to an area that's off limits, say so. We'll keep on walking while we talk, so I'll have to keep half an eye on things around us. Some nasty beasties in this waste and we wouldn't want to walk into any of them unaware."

It was obvious. Anything that had to do with the Vyinnlyirr of the waste was blocked. Which meant that in a normal state Thassyil must have known something of them! Which in turn meant that the Leader, Thryimm and the Keeper of Memories had all been lying about the Others. But why? What purpose did it serve?

The issue of the reason for the Call wasn't blocked. Thassyil simply didn't have the foggiest notion. But Seeker couldn't help but feel the two were one and the same. How did the Vyinnlyirr in the waste relate to the Call?

There was another area blocked which puzzled Seeker

greatly. Any access to information about the flickers or the degeneration of the crystal was very limited. Thassyil could admit both were happening, but could not assign any importance to either. Nor could the Vyinnlyirr give any account as to the cause. Could this also be a clue?

The surprise was that the very idea of the Others was doubly blocked! They had worked past the block that referred to the Vyinnlyirr in the waste. But there was a further block which, once the existence of Others in the waste was admitted, closed down any further discussion of the idea. Why?

The Novice trudged along, half sunk in thought, half alert to the waste. The long talk with Thassyil had made things more confusing rather than less. But at least if it ever got back to the city, it knew where to start.

The waste seemed endless. Every ridge was like every other. All looked out over a prospect that was bleak and desolate. The sand sucked at the feet, holding them, making walking a difficult and almost painful task. The worst thing, though, was the cold. It sapped the energy and tired one even more than the treacherous sand. No matter how tightly Seeker wrapped the cloak around itself, it was never warm enough.

In the last two days, the barriers between Seeker and its host had almost completely broken down. They had become friends and companions in the most intimate sense. Somehow they had managed to work it so that both were always conscious most of the time and both inhabited the body fully. This made things easier, since Thassyil was much more adept at using its body than Seeker. Also, senses the Vyinnlyirr had not used before came out and made their stumbling through the waste safer and surer. They were working as a team now.

They stopped at the top of a ridge and gazed around. Off toward the east, the sun was halfway up toward noon. The sand was swirling more than usual, for a brisk wind blew from the northwest and swept it along in hissing streams. The ridge they stood on was solid rock. Seeker noted that it appeared of volcanic origin. Indeed, most of the exposed rock in the waste seemed of that type.

The waste was a strange and frightening place. It seemed so simple at first glance. Sand, gravel, a few rocks, wind, some plants, a few animals, nothing much. Nothing at all like the richness and complexity of the planet where Seeker had been raised. The Novice thought longingly of the lush grass and frequent streams of the plain. So much food, so much water. It had never appreciated it enough.

Even Labyrinth was a paradise compared to this empty waste. Probably no more dangerous, either. There, it was true, the planet was sentient and tried to kill you. Here there was no sentience. Just the brute fact of a dead world with no water and no food. There was no way to outthink the waste. Quick reflexes didn't help. One had to watch where one stepped, of course. But it was the waste itself that was the danger, not the rare creatures that populated it.

Here and there, Seeker knew, there had to be entrances to the tunnels of the Vyinnlyirr. They were hidden, of course. And probably guarded as well. They could be standing within a few feet of one of them and not even know it. But there would be water there. And food. If only . . .

The waste. Emptiness. Simplicity. And yet not so simple after all. Everything changed constantly, Seeker realized. The sand blew endlessly, shifting constantly. One day a dune would be there. The next it would be gone. There was no way to follow landmarks in this waste because they changed hour by hour. It was a vast labyrinth of its own. But one that constantly transformed itself, making itself anew every day, reshuffling the same simple elements in infinite variety.

What would H*mb*l do in a case like this? Dance the waste? But that wouldn't be possible. Dancing was not enough in this case, for the dance of the waste was the dance of death. No, even H*mb*l could not deal with this.

Bilrog? The Furmorian warrior was a tower of strength and could struggle on long after Seeker had dropped in its tracks. Yes, Bilrog would battle this waste with all its tremendous power. And it would lose. The power of the waste was infinite, and Bilrog's counterforce was miniscule in comparison.

Longarm, then. Surely the Teacher would know what to do. Seeker tried to image Longarm shambling through the waste. It brought a chuckle to the Novice's lips, but the image was not a pleasant one. Longarm, too, would die here. Indeed, as the Teacher had said many times, the universe was filled with death and no one should be surprised to meet up with it.

How then will I fare? Seeker wondered. We'll die, Thassyil interjected gloomily. We'll die out here together.

Seeker snorted. Not yet, we won't, it stated grimly. Not for a couple more days. We've still got enough strength left for a couple more days. We'll keep going until we drop. And then we'll crawl. I want to get back to that city, Seeker said with sudden ferocity. And, by all my protoeggs, we're damn well going to give it our best!

A vast boulder field stretched off toward the horizon. I don't remember this, Seeker admitted. We didn't come through this on the way out. But then, it added before Thassyil could despair, we might be north or south of our original path and still be dead on target.

They stood and stared for some time at the boulders. Not easy to work one's way through that, Seeker admitted. Hard, thirsty work. And we have no water or food left. Well, at least that makes us lighter.

The boulders were strewn every which way, tumbled in chaotic confusion. Some were huge, fully fifty feet through. Others were only a few feet across. Most were of the same black, volcanic rock the made up most of the waste. Here and there, though, odd-colored rocks showed, some blood red, others deep green, and now and then a dirty yellow one. The air over the boulder field was still and heavy. The whole area seemed even more desolate than the open sand dunes and rocky ridges they had been crossing.

Seeker shrugged and started down the hill toward the boulders. Things could be hiding in there, Thassyil warned. Seems like the perfect place for an ambush.

What could ambush us out here? Seeker asked. There isn't a living thing within . . .

The lizard leapt from the left, where it had been hiding at the base of a boulder. Thassyil had seen the slight motion as the lizard gathered its strength to attack and had thrown its body forward into a roll. The thing's jaws snapped on a piece of the robe and black poison spewed over the cloth, making it smoke. Seeker whipped out its knives and slashed quickly downward, hitting the lizard just behind the head. The thing hissed and let go. It struck the ground, its legs already going full speed for a second attack. Thassyil threw its body to one side and Seeker flung the knives to meet the creature in midair. Both hit with a solid thunk. The lizard hit the ground, twitched for a few moments and then died.

Quick, Thassyil commanded, cut off the head before the

poison gets back into the body. Without thinking, Seeker sprang to the task, slicing the head with several swift slashes. Then it held the lizard up by its tail, allowing the blood to drain out.

When they had both caught their breath, Seeker spoke aloud to Thassyil. "How did you know to cut the head off?"

The Vyinnlyirr paused in surprise. "I . . . I don't know. I just did. It sort of came to me in a flash. This lizard has huge poison glands behind its front legs. When it attacks, the poison surges forward into the fangs. Gives it lots of the stuff that way, more than it would have if the poison was in the head alone. If you don't cut the head off right away after it strikes, the poison goes back into the body and the thing's not fit to eat. I . . . I don't know how I knew that."

Seeker considered. "Blocked. It was part of the blocked memories, Thassyil. In the excitement and stress, you somehow managed to tap into it. Maybe your mind is getting worried about its survival and is fighting the blocks. I don't know.

"But the point is, you do have knowledge of the waste and the creatures in it! It's there in your mind."

"But why, Questioner? What good could such knowledge do an inhabitant of the city?"

"I don't know, yet," Seeker replied grimly. "But it has saved us for the moment. We have food and some water in this lizard. Our chances of making it back have just gone way up, Thassyil. And when we do get back, we're going to find out just why you have knowledge that would only make sense for a Vyinnlyirr of the waste to have."

Together, they set about cutting the lizard apart into pieces small enough to swallow. The taste was disgusting, but this time Thassyil did not become sick. When they had finished, they stood and began to thread their weary way through the boulder field.

XIII.

"Why did they want to kill us?" Seeker asked as it stumbled along across the sand. "Why did the Vyinnlyirr of the waste try to kill us?"

"They didn't try very hard," Thassyil mumbled in reply. "And they didn't try to kill 'us.' They only wanted you out of the way. I just happen to be the package you come in."

"Sorry," the Novice replied. "Not my choice. But you're wrong about not trying very hard. The attack with the knives wasn't particularly expertly done, I grant. Of course, if I'd been asleep it could have proven fatal. But I don't really think it was meant to be. I think they would have made enough noise first to make sure I was awake. No, I think they wanted us to escape, Thassyil. Escape into the waste. After all, why kill a Questioner yourself when you have something as effective as the waste to do it for you? No possible repercussions that way. Poor, stupid Questioner just wandered off into the waste and died. As normal and natural as the sun rising. But why?"

Thassyil failed to reply and they trudged along in thoughtful silence for several moments. Then Seeker had another idea. "For that matter, I guess I could say that the willingness of Thryimm and the Leader to send me out into the waste in the first place was a form of murder. I had become an embarrassment to them and they knew precisely what would happen if I came out here. Thryimm intimated as much."

"But why call a Questioner and then just kill it?"

"I don't know. I don't even know why I was called in the first place. At first I thought it was something to do with the slow breakdown of the city. When Lissyi showed me the deterioration, I thought I understood at last. But then it told me the process would take tens of thousands of years. So that couldn't be the reason. Then I thought it had to have something to do with the Others. But I'm not sure that's it either, especially since the mysterious Others turned out to be nothing but more Vyinnlyirr. It just doesn't make sense, Thassyil."

"Over there to the left," Thassyil said suddenly, its voice tense with fear. Seeker pulled its knives out instantly and spun to face the indicated direction, crouched in a fighting stance.

"What?" the Novice asked, seeing nothing at all that seemed dangerous.

"There, buried in the sand, about twenty-five feet away, near that rock."

"I don't see any..." Then Seeker realized what it was looking at. "Wheeeewww!" it whistled. "Good spotting, Thassyil. Damn, one of those lizards again. The kind that bite and paralyze. I can just see its head. Damn. Looks like a small rock."

Thassyil shivered in fear. "Let's go."

Seeker shook its head. "No. It's food, Thassyil. And a source of moisture. I'm feeling very hungry and damnably thirsty. Another day without food or water and we'll be in trouble. Right now I still have enough strength and speed to have a chance against that thing. Tomorrow or the next day, it'll have the upper hand. I want to kill it and eat it now, Thassyil."

"It's fast," Thassyil whimpered.

"If you're too afraid, just crawl back out of the way and leave it to me."

Thassyil thought a moment. "No," it finally said. "No, you could use my help. You'll be faster with me than without. I'll stay."

"Good," Seeker replied. "We'll walk directly toward it. I think it likes to attack from the side since it probably has less of a chance of being seen in advance that way. Our best bet is from the front."

Slowly they walked toward the buried lizard, tense and ready, watching for the slightest move on the part of the deadly creature. When they were only ten feet from the thing, Seeker paused, unsure how much closer to come. At what point would they no longer have adequate time to react when it . . .

It exploded from the sand, a blur of motion. Seeker whipped both of the knives forward, flinging them directly at the charging lizard, throwing itself as far to the right as it could at the same instant. One of the knives struck, but the other skittered harmlessly across the sand. The lizard was wounded, but hardly dead. Seeker scrambled to its feet and clawed its third weapon, the strangely shaped knife/axe, from where it was tucked inside the robe. As the lizard sprang for them once more, Seeker threw again. The weapon slashed the creature, leaving a gaping wound on its left side, but it failed to stick or kill.

The lizard was slower now, but still deadly. It moved cautiously, sizing up its opponent with care. Seeker backed away, trying to keep at least ten feet between them. The thing lunged and hurled itself at Seeker. The Novice flung itself sideways and hit the ground rolling to give even greater distance. It sprang back to its feet once more. The lizard was already springing. Seeker dodged and spun, barely avoiding the poisonous fangs.

Seeker took several quick steps away from the beast. How long before it wears out? the Novice wondered. Not enough time, Thassyil wailed in response. But it's wounded, Seeker pointed out. Not badly enough, Thassyil replied. We'll wear out before it does.

The Novice snorted in anger at its host's pessimism. Die trying, it said to the Vyinnlyirr, grunting as it spun away from a new attack. Die, cried Thassyil miserably, oh, die, die . . . Seeker felt the Vyinnlyirr slink off into its hiding place.

The lizard stalked forward, trying to close the gap between them. Seeker backpedaled to keep it open. Suddenly the Novice's foot caught on a rock and it lost its balance. At the same instant, sensing its prey's dilemma, the lizard attacked. Seeker fell and rolled as fast as it could. The lizard missed and spun around for another try.

As it rolled, Seeker felt a strange shape beneath its body. Instantly recognizing it, the Novice grabbed it and scrambled to its knees. As the lizard sprang, Seeker hurled the knife/axe straight into the beast's face. It caught the creature right in the mouth, which was open for the kill. The metal smashed and cut the thing's head nearly in two, and it fell twitching within a foot of the kneeling Novice.

Seeker felt the strength drain from its body. It collapsed sideways on the sand, gasping for breath. Couldn't stand if I wanted to, it realized. "Hey, Thassyil," it crowed out loud, "we won!"

Thassyil peeped out of its hiding place. "Won? We . . . you killed it?"

"Damn right," Seeker said aloud. "Any poison glands in this thing that have to be cut out?"

"None that I know of," Thassyil said meekly. "We can just eat it as it is. But not the head. That's the bad part."

Between mouthfuls, Seeker said, "I was just thinking of something, Thassyil."

"Don't you ever stop thinking, Questioner?" Thassyil replied with a sigh. "Not even when you're eating?"

Seeker chuckled. "It's dangerous to stop thinking in a place like this waste, Thassyil. But I was thinking of something else, something strange. This lizard, to be precise."

"What's so strange about it?"

"Well, not just about it, but about it and you Vyinnlyirr. This thing is a native of this planet, right? And you are not. So this thing and its poison were not designed to paralyze creatures with metabolisms like yours. Yet that is exactly what happens. It bites you and the poison paralyzes you, just the way it would paralyze a species that had developed right here in the waste along with this creature. Now I can understand how its poison might kill you. Bizarre proteins and all that. But why would it have precisely the same effect on you Vyinnlyirr as it has on a native species? You've been here a while, but not long enough for that kind of evolutionary convergence."

"Coincidence?" Thassyil suggested.

"Possibly," Seeker shrugged, "but it seems like an awfully long shot to me."

"So what do you think it means?"

"I don't really know," Seeker sighed. "It's just one more mystery to this place. It probably doesn't mean anything at all, but . . . There are so many pieces to this puzzle that just don't seem to fit together to make any sensible pattern."

"Maybe you're looking for something that isn't there."

"Oh, it's there," Seeker replied. "Sentience, unless it's arachnid sentience, always has a pattern. Things make sense. I just can't seem to get my head wrapped around this one, that's all." Seeker sighed again. "Just have to keep trying."

For two days they trudged across the waste without seeing another living creature. In every direction the sand and gravel rose and fell in solid waves of desolation. The silence was total except for the crunch, crunch of their steps and the malevolent hiss of the wind hurrying the sand here and there.

The emptiness began to prey on Thassyil's mind. The Vyinnlyirr was used to living in the city. And although the Vyinnlyirr in the city were not notably gregarious, there were always some around if company was desired. Here Thassyil was utterly alone, completely cut off from its own kind. Slowly it retreated deeper and deeper into its own mind.

Seeker felt the desolation almost as sharply as its host. The vast indifference of the waste ate away at the Novice's confidence in a way that was far more destructive, if more subtle, than the way Labyrinth had. At least on Labyrinth, Seeker thought, there was usually something to fight against, some beast that attacked. Here there is virtually nothing coherent and identifiable to struggle with. The waste itself was too vast and neutral to be a true opponent. And yet, the Novice realized, it was by far the deadliest enemy it had ever met.

The fourth day after eating the lizard, they began to weaken rapidly. The landscape had turned to gravel again, and walking was more difficult and painful than ever. The gravel slipped and rolled out from beneath the Vyinnlyirr feet, and they fell many times. Each time, getting back up was harder and harder.

"Questioner," Thassyil finally moaned, "I . . . I can't go any further."

Seeker nodded. "Your Vyinnlyirr body isn't very strong. No offense, but I'd much rather be in my own body right now. We . . . last a lot longer. But if you can't go on, Thassyil, just go to sleep or something. I'm not through yet. If I have to crawl across this damn waste, inch by inch, I'm making it back to the city." Suiting action to words, Seeker forced the Vyinnlyirr body to its feet one more time.

Thassyil was silent for some time, but Seeker knew the

Vyinnlyirr was still there and had not gone to sleep or retreated into its own corner. Finally it spoke. "Won't they rescue you at some point? I mean, won't they come for you or something? Can't you just go back the way you came?"

It was Seeker's turn to be silent. "I'm really not sure. I . . . don't think so. First of all, there isn't any 'them' somewhere checking on how I'm doing. Only a computer that's monitoring my mind. And I really don't know exactly what it's monitoring or looking for. I can't really call it. It just knows . . . well, it's supposed to know, when I've finished the mission. Until then, it just leaves me alone."

"But isn't your mission over? We . . . we're going to die here, both of us, unless you leave. If . . . if you go back, only one of us will die. I . . ."

"I'm not going anywhere," Seeker promised. "I'm not going to abandon you here in the waste, Thassyil. If we die, then *we* die. But I have no intention of dying. I'm going to make it back to the city and you're coming with me."

Thassyil was thoughtfully silent for several moments. When it finally spoke, its voice was subdued but firm. "I . . . I guess I'll keep on as well, then. You could probably use my help."

"Glad to have you," Seeker replied. "It's always easier when we work together. You still know a lot more about this body, and this waste, than I do. It'll be a lot easier to stay alive if we work on it together."

"Ummm," Thassyil mused as they staggered along. "And if we're going to die, it might be easier to die together."

They had lost count of the number of times they had fallen and then slowly, painfully struggled back to their feet. Even time became a bleary concept and they stumbled through the dark just as they did through the light. "Got to be near," Seeker mumbled. "Gone enough days. Near. See it soon."

"Can't see well. Eyes tired," Thassyil croaked weakly. "Miss it. Stumbled right by it."

"Too big," Seeker declared. "Can't miss it." But when it tried to look off into the distance through the Vyinnlyirr's eyes, it realized that indeed the creature's eyesight was failing.

Crawling now from time to time. Falling down and not able to rise, then crawling for a while until they came to a rock or something to help pull themselves upright. Stumbling and staggering all the time. Reeling across the gravel and sand like a cub just learning to walk. Falling, crawling.

The thirst was a burning in the throat and beak, a longing that distracted the mind. Hunger was a dull ache that never let one alone. Together they battered and dulled the mind, weakening it and distracting it. Things were hard to follow. There was no way to track a reasoned argument. Seeker had simply stopped thinking in order to concentrate all its efforts on surviving. It was hard enough to walk, to place one foot in front of the other, to fall, to crawl, then to rise eventually and plod along again.

Cold, so cold. Right foot, left foot. Cramps in the stomach. Bend over as if to hug them. They don't stop any more. Tongue swollen and painful, hot like a fiery worm bulging out of the beak. Can't see right any more. Things wiggle and move, shift and darken unpredictably. Right foot, left foot.

So quiet. Hiss of wind. Crunch-slide of foot. Quiet as death. Death. Dying. Tongue hanging out, parched, swollen, pain red in the head. Stumble and smash face down against the rocks, cut, bleeding. Struggle up, lurch onward.

Eyes clouded. Breath short. Shorter. Panting now. It hurts when I breathe. Cold. So cold.

Crawling. Can't stand. Hands, knees raw. Eyes blind. Crawling forward. Lost. Dying.

Dying.

Dying.

Too weak to move. Lying face down. Grit against the beak, in the mouth, on the tongue. Cold. Dark.

Hand stretches out to grab the ground, pull the body one inch closer to safety. Rational thought long gone. Instinct now. Running down. Still fighting. Pull an inch at a time.

Too weak to move. Put the hand out slowly, fingers twitching. Grab, pull. Too weak.

No more motion now. Still. The dark comes. And the cold.

The sun rose and shone bleakly on the unmoving bundle of rags. One arm was thrust out toward the city that towered, glowing with morning light, only a few yards away. The fingers on the hand were splayed out in one last attempt to grab the earth and hold tight. But the hand was still, empty.

The hiss of the wind was the loudest noise to be heard on the waste.

"It looks like a bundle of rags."

"What would a bundle of rags be doing in the waste?"

"I don't know. Perhaps we should tell the Leader."

A shrug. "I doubt it affects the Project. What difference does it make? One bundle of rags?"

"But outside? In the waste? What in the name of light and air are rags doing in the waste? I'm going that way. I'll tell the Leader."

"Should we?" the Leader asked.

"Perhaps it would be best to drop the whole matter. This seems a satisfactory solution to me," Thryimm answered.

"But we made the Call for a purpose."

Thryimm shrugged. "Perhaps we misunderstood. I don't think we need a Questioner."

The Leader nodded firmly. "Oh, yes, a Questioner is very necessary. Very."

Thryimm sighed. "Very well, then, I'll go out and get the fool. Where do you think it's been all this time? Just wandering around in circles? What do you suppose it found out there in the waste? I'm really amazed to see it again after so long." Thryimm turned and left without waiting for an answer to its questions.

The Leader stood brooding as it stared out at the shape that lay crumpled in a heap near the base of the city. "Hopefully," it finally said, so softly that even someone standing a few feet away couldn't have heard, "it found what it was supposed to find."

In the Abyss

*Whoever fights monsters
should see to it that in the process
he does not become a monster.
And when you look long into an abyss,
the abyss also looks into you.*

Friedrich Nietzsche,
Beyond Good and Evil

XIV.

Thryimm shook its head in disbelief. "That's absurd! Nothing can live out there, especially not the Children of Light and Air. You must have been suffering from delusion, Questioner. The cold, the hunger and thirst, the desolation. Delirium brought on by such a close shave with death. Yes, that must be it."

Seeker fixed Thryimm with a hard glare. "Thassyil wants me to tell you that you are a fool, Thryimm. We were gone for more than thirty days. When we left the city, we carried food and water for no more than five. How do you account for our ability to survive if our story is not true?"

The Leader chuckled. "I fear they have a point there, Thryimm. Stop staring at them so stupidly. They both agree there are Vyinnlyirr in the waste and I don't see any way to deny what they have claimed. Especially since their knowledge comes from experience and ours from mere conjecture about what happened thousands of years ago. Vyinnlyirr in the waste! My. Who would have thought? But it does seem to make sense of some things we didn't understand. Precisely where did you find them, Questioner?"

The Novice smiled slowly. "I didn't. They found us. And they are very worried, or claim to be, that you might wish them harm, so they went to great pains to disguise the openings to their tunnels and to keep us from figuring out where we were. I really haven't the slightest idea where they are, except that they lie many days into the waste toward the setting sun.

"They are afraid of us?" trilled the Leader with high humor. "Why, what in the name of the Project do they think we could want with them? They have nothing we need. And they certainly pose no threat to us. We are dedicated to the Project. We are turned inward toward ourselves, not outward toward a few scruffy survivors clinging to a pitiful existence in the far reaches of the waste! What an amusing idea, don't you think, Thryimm!?"

Thryimm nodded vaguely, clearly unsure yet as to exactly what it thought. "Of course. No interest. Foolish of them," the Vyinnlyirr muttered.

"Well, Questioner," the Leader said expansively, "relax, recuperate. Everything you need is right here in Thassyil's nest. And if there's anything you want, don't hesitate to let Thryimm or me know. Yes, you'll be fine again in a few days. Good as new. Yes, good as new and twice as inquisitive, eh?" With that, the Leader and Thryimm displayed their membranes and swept from the nest. But just before the Leader turned away, Seeker could have sworn it winked ever so subtly.

The city was a place transformed. When Seeker was well enough to walk through it once more, everywhere it went it met Vyinnlyirr walking along in groups, in pairs, or alone. Some were striding purposefully and merely nodded in passing. Others stopped to talk and compliment Thassyil and Seeker on their adventure. Every now and then, they would come across a single Vyinnlyirr or a group that was standing gazing off into the lucent distance and trilling some eerie but beautiful song.

Everywhere Seeker wandered, the light seemed to be brighter than before and the very air was rich with the sounds and sense of the Vyinnlyirr. The city, which had been so deserted and cold, was now bustling and filled with warm life.

"This," Thassyil informed Seeker, "is the way it usually is. Everyone going about doing their part of the Project, singing, calling to each other, full of light and air." Thassyil's sense of pride was strong.

"Why was it so empty before?" the Novice asked.

"They were all unsure. The Leader asked everyone to stay off the streets at first. We weren't too sure how you would adapt and wanted to give you time to get used to the city and being in a Vyinnlyirr body before you had to get used to all the rest of us as well. It was a question of courtesy, you know."

"Courtesy? I wonder," Seeker mused, nodding to a group of several Vyinnlyirr that were passing as they crossed a long bridge of pale yellow crystal that stretched across a vast chasm filled with bluish-green light. "Those I met at that time, Thassyil, the blind Lissyi and Syllini the Mad One, were they also part of the courtesy? Did they come of their own, or were they sent? Was Lissyi even blind or Syllini even mad?"

"Lissyi is blind, I can assure you of that. And Syllini was considered mad, though I admit its recovery among the Vyinnlyirr of the waste was nothing short of miraculous. Although I can't say for sure, I imagine their meetings with you were their own ideas. They were both . . . a little odd. Not likely to follow orders, if you know what I mean."

"Thassyil, one of the best ways to get a young cub to do what you want is to order it to do exactly the opposite. That's something every Nurturer learns very early in its phase."

Thassyil shrugged mentally. "Of course that's possible. But why go to all the trouble? We have nothing to hide."

"Nothing? No, you hide nothing. But you also show nothing. Or perhaps what you do show is pointing in exactly the opposite direction from the one in which I should be looking. All the Vyinnlyirr are back in the streets. There is so much to see here that one could spend many days just walking around looking."

"An excellent idea, Questioner. You will gain a good deal of understanding of the Vyinnlyirr by watching us in our natural state, working on the Project, trilling out songs of light, or joy, or discovery. Yes, you will learn much."

"I think that's exactly what the Leader would like me to think. Myself, I think I will learn nothing of interest. The finger points too clearly in one direction. I will look in the other. Thassyil, I want to go back down to the base of the city. I want to find Lissyi again."

The sand-filled ways at the base of the city were empty and deserted. From above, the sounds of the Children of Light and Air filtered down, echoing oddly, a ghostly reminder that elsewhere there was life and activity.

"What is beneath all this, Thassyil?"

"You mean below the base of the city? Well, I'm not too

sure. I suppose it's the machinery that maintains the city. The energy generators, the air machines, the equipment that manufactures food and water, things like that. But I'm not sure. I've never really heard anyone talk about it."

"So you've come back," a voice trilled softly behind them. Thassyil jumped mentally, but Seeker turned slowly and casually. "Hello, Lissyi. I thought you might be here."

"The word is warbled from every tower: 'The Questioner has returned with Thassyil from the waste! They have found the Others and they are Vyinnlyirr!' I knew sooner or later you would come down here once more. So I have waited."

"Lissyi," Seeker asked, "what is beneath the city?"

The blind Vyinnlyirr paused thoughtfully. "Ah, ah, yes, beneath the city. Lissyi knew you would ask that sooner or later, yes, yes."

Lissyi came closer to the Novice and stared at it with blind eyes. Its voice was a soft hiss. "Beneath the city is a vast abyss, a yawning chasm that some say reaches down, down to the very heart of this planet. It is from there the city draws its power, power that will last as long as this world endures, eons and eons. Can't you feel the beating of that heart, Questioner? The throbbing, trembling beat that makes the very ground you stand on vibrate?

"And there in the abyss is a vast labyrinth, a maze of tunnels giving access to the machinery that keeps this city functioning. Machines that tear the energy from the heart of our planet and transform it into light and heat and food and air for the Children of Light and Air.

"But the abyss is dark and terrifying and empty. None go there. None dare. For it enters the mind and drains it of hope and light and air. Yes, yes, the abyss! Under all this light and glory, Questioner, lies a horrible dark and empty gape, a nothingness so profound it shrivels the soul and mind!"

Seeker sighed. "So in less poetic terms, Lissyi, there's a lot of machinery and tunnels and a tap to the center of the planet for geothermal energy, right?"

Lissyi stepped back in surprise. "It is not that cut and dried, Questioner. The abyss is very real and horrible. It . . ."

"I'm sure it is, Lissyi. How can I get below the surface to investigate the machinery?"

The Blind One gasped and lifted its hands in horror. Thassyil squawked a mental protest. Seeker ignored their reactions. "I'd

City of Crystal Shadow

like to have a look at the machinery. I haven't seen any of the mysterious flickers since we returned, Thassyil, but I haven't forgotten them. They must be a result of some sort of malfunctioning of the machinery. I'd like to see it."

"Are you ... are you some kind of engineer on your home world, Questioner?" Lissyi asked with obvious respect.

"No," the Novice replied smoothly. "I have no intention of fixing the machinery. I wouldn't have the slightest idea how to go about it."

"But then why ... ?"

"I don't know why. It just seems like a good idea."

"There is no access to the abyss," the Leader declared firmly.

"Just as there was none to the waste?" Seeker replied, a slight edge of sarcasm sharpening its tone.

"The waste is different, Questioner. As you already know, although we don't like to think about it, there are those Vyinnlyirr who go mad and flee to the waste. So there is need of access, even though we don't make it generally known it exists. Indeed, as you discovered, we even try to hide it.

"But the abyss is different. It is filled with nothing but the machinery that runs the city. And that machinery runs and maintains itself automatically. There is no need for any Vyinnlyirr to ever go that far from the light and air. The abyss was sealed when the city was completed. No access was provided because none was needed."

"And yet the flickers indicate there are problems with the machinery. Aren't any of you curious to look and see if there is something that might be done?"

The Leader shrugged. "Curious? Why? We spend our time on the Project. The whole city, including the machinery that runs it and the very abyss in which it was placed, were created for the sole purpose of the Project. We know nothing of the machinery, nor do we need to. It flickers now and then, true, but it is a minor thing, and as long as it does not disrupt the Project there is nothing to worry about. Besides, none of us would know how to fix it anyway."

"And what if the flickers become something more than minor? What if they become major? What if they disrupt the Project?"

"That ... that is inconceivable!"

"Is it really? Isn't the Project powered by the machines? Of course it is. And if the power should fail in a significant way, might not part of the Project be harmed in some fashion?"

"No! That could not happen! It is . . . please leave now, Questioner. You . . . you have upset me! To speak of harm coming to the Project . . . ! I must regain my calm, for I have many things to do on the Project. Leave now!"

Seeker lifted its membranes and turned to leave. When it was halfway out of the room, a flicker came. First a bare ripple in the light. Then a sudden stopping of everything, light dimming, airflow halting, the eternal background hum falling silent. There was a vast groan that rose into the still air, a groan that came from the very crystal of the city itself. Then, just as suddenly as it had come, the flicker passed.

The Novice turned and looked at the Leader. The Vyinnlyirr was standing rigidly, its eyes stricken with surprise, its beak open in shock. Seeker nodded pleasantly. "Inconceivable," it said simply, and then turned and left.

"There must be access here somewhere, Thassyil," Seeker said. "But it won't be any more obvious than the access to the waste."

"There is no reason to go into the abyss," Thassyil declared, its thoughts clouded by fear.

Seeker paused in its search and asked softly, "Why are you so afraid of the abyss, Thassyil? You've survived the waste. Can the abyss be so much worse?"

"Yesssss," hissed the Vyinnlyirr. "Yessss, much, much worse! The waste is empty of all but the most deadly of life, Questioner. It is a harsh, cold place of death and pain. But it is still filled with glorious light and flowing air!

"But the abyss! The abyss is dark, empty, endless. And the air there is close and suffocating, dead and still. It is . . . it is the most horrible place a Vyinnlyirr can imagine! It terrifies me, Questioner, in a much deeper and more profound way than ever the waste did. I would . . . I would fear for my sanity there." Thassyil's voice trailed off into a tense whisper in the mind they shared.

"But we wouldn't need a long trip, Thassyil," Seeker said, trying to calm its host. "It would be nothing like going into the waste. Just a quick look at the machines. We'd take light with us. Only a matter of a few hours at most."

"The machinery is vast, Questioner," Thassyil replied, its voice quivering with fright. "The tunnels are a labyrinth one could become lost in and wander through forever, buried in the dark. I fear it, Questioner! I fear it more than anything in this world!"

"Well," the Novice said, trying to mollify Thassyil, "we won't make any firm plans, then. We'll just try to find an access and then see what happens. Sort of play it by ear, so to speak."

Thassyil mumbled and retreated into its corner. Seeker sighed and realized it would have to continue the search alone. But to itself, hiding the thought from Thassyil, it wondered how the Vyinnlyirr knew so much about the abyss if no one had ever been there.

It was more than a flicker this time. It was the middle of the night when the lights died, the air stopped, and the whole city shook and clanged. The darkness crashed down, hiding the soaring spires and bridges from view. Vyinnlyirr fled through the streets in panic or fell into whimpering heaps.

It lasted for at least five minutes. Then the lights slowly came back on, dim and wavering at first, then gradually growing in strength. The air began to move and the usual hum filled the air once more. But the Vyinnlyirr stood or lay where they were, their eyes dazed and frightened, unsure of what they should do next.

Suddenly a siren went off and they all came back to life in an instant, rushing off in all directions with horrified and agonized cries. "The Project!" Thassyil shouted to Seeker. "Something's happened to the Project!"

XV.

"A minor problem," the Leader said. Then it shivered. "Only a minor loss of data. We had backup files of the material lost, and they will be read into the main file again. Minor. But disquieting, Questioner. Yes, disquieting."

Seeker nodded. "I take it this is not the first time this has happened?"

"What makes you say that?" Thryimm asked sharply, its voice suspicious.

"Because," Seeker answered smoothly, "you have the drill down so well. The siren sounds and everyone rushes to their stations to see what has happened. And you have backup files to cover just such an emergency. Redundancy in systems, Thryimm, is a technique that only occurs to those who have experienced loss before."

The Leader nodded solemnly. "Of course you are correct, Questioner. This has happened before. But only very rarely. The Project is protected by many layers of redundancy. It is very carefully thought out."

"Why are the machines failing, Leader?" Seeker asked point-blank. "There must be a reason."

The Leader gave a deep sigh and turned to Thryimm. "I think this is your question. You should answer it."

Thryimm looked grimly at the Leader. "I don't think we should reveal this information. Not even to a Questioner."

"I disagree. Would you like to ask for a higher ruling?"

Thryimm paused, then sighed. "No. That won't be necessary." The Vyinnlyirr turned to Seeker and gave the Novice a sour look. "Questioner," Thryimm began, "my task is that of security for the Project."

"Somehow," Seeker said ironically, "I'm not really surprised. It seems that military men of all species are rather similar."

Thryimm gave the Novice an unreadable look and then continued. "My task as head of security is to be sure nothing, absolutely nothing, interferes with the smooth running of the Project."

"And something is interfering?"

"Yes, something is interfering."

"Something that causes the flickers?"

"Thryimm nodded glumly. "Yes. Precisely. It is not a question of the machines deteriorating and breaking down. It is rather a matter of sabotage."

Seeker was surprised. "Sabotage? But who would sabotage . . ."

"The Others," Thryimm said softly. "The *real* Others."

The Novice stared at Thryimm. "Then there *are* Others? I mean, not just the Vyinnlyirr of the waste?"

Thryimm nodded. "Yes. The Others are the original inhabitants of this planet, even as you heard the very first time you asked about them."

"But I thought they all died when you closed them out of the city."

"True. Or at least partly true. Those we closed out died. But those we kept here with us did not."

"You kept some of them here in the city with you? Where are they? Do they still exist?"

Thryimm nodded grimly. "Oh, yes, they still exist. Or at least a few of them do. They were kept in the city to help run it. They were trained to maintain the machinery. They were put into the abyss and given that task."

"So the abyss is inhabited?"

"Yes, inhabited," the Leader said. "The Others were put there to keep the machinery in good condition. It was their part of the Project, their mission. For many thousands of years they performed their part well. But then something happened."

"They began to degenerate." Thryimm took up the tale. "They lost sight of the role they played in the Project and wanted to come out of the abyss into the city. They called it 'freedom.'" Thryimm's voice was heavy with disgust. "As if there was any freedom other than in serving the Project.

"Naturally, we rejected their requests and sealed most of the accessways to the abyss. The rest we put locks on and guarded carefully. At first they tried to escape and a few battles were fought. They were no match for us, for we had all the resources of the city at our command. We defeated them and threw them back into the abyss where they belonged.

"For many years after their defeat, which had been truly crushing, we had no problems with them. Then another generation of leaders arose making foolish new demands. They wanted to go out of the city, back onto the surface of the planet, back to what they called their homeland."

"But of course," the Leader said, "that was impossible. Their homeland was gone, their planet destroyed to build the city. There was only the waste. They were not adapted to live there. They would have perished miserably there."

"We pointed that out to them, in all kindness and consideration," Thryimm continued. "But they stubbornly refused to pay heed. Once more they tried to break out of the abyss. The only course open to us was to seal all the accessways and lock them permanently below the city. We hoped this would bring them to their senses and make them see that their mission was to fulfill their role as maintainers of the machinery."

"It all went well for a time," the Leader said thoughtfully. "Everything ran smoothly. But then the flickers began to happen. At first we were uncertain what was wrong. We checked the remote readouts and could find no malfunctions. Then we realized what was happening. The Others were purposely causing problems, purposely sabotaging the machinery to cause the flickers!"

"Luckily," Thryimm said, "the machinery is self-repairing. Most of the things they do are minor and can be fixed by the machines themselves. But over the years, their destructiveness began to mount and caused more serious problems. Like the one you recently witnessed. We feared for the very Project itself.

"We realized something had to be done. It was distasteful,

but we came to the inevitable conclusion that we would have to punish the Others severely to bring them back to their senses and to their mission.

"So we sent security forces into the abyss. We fought them and destroyed many of them. Our victory was almost complete."

"Almost complete," echoed the Leader thoughtfully. "But not quite. They had learned many things during the first conflict. And leaders of unusual skill and cleverness had arisen among them. They split into many small groups and scattered among the endless tunnels that lie within the abyss. The task of hunting them all down, group by group, was impossible. We smashed any large force whenever we met one that stood and fought, but the smaller groups would retreat as we advanced and then as we turned away, they would strike from behind or circle around and attack from ambush. It was an endless conflict, draining, foolish, wasteful."

"We tried negotiation, even offered to let them go out onto the surface. But their whole goal had changed. Now, rather than their stupid 'freedom,' they wanted revenge. They wanted to destroy the city and wreck the Project. They hated us, the Project, the city, the light and air, everything beautiful and good. They became true creatures of the dark abyss. There was no compromise possible with them.

"Annihilation was the only answer. Reluctantly we set about it. One by one, we hunted down the groups and their leaders. One by one we destroyed them."

The Leader sighed. "It was an endless task, as you can imagine, Questioner. The vermin multiplied almost as fast as we could exterminate them. But then we realized that the best plan was to capture or kill their leaders, for without leaders they were relatively harmless. A mere nuisance rather than a real threat." The Leader paused, a thoughtful look crossing its face. "It seemed to work for a while."

"For a while," Thryimm replied. "Yes, for a while. But the only way to rid ourselves of this problem is to annihilate them all. As long as even one of them exists, new leaders will grow up among them. We must exterminate them all!"

The Leader nodded sadly at Thryimm. "I know your views quite well, Thryimm. And I still feel they are too harsh. To exterminate the entire race . . . well, that's too much. I would rather bring them back to their mission. We still need them to maintain the machinery and help run the city. It would be best for the Project if . . ."

"If they were all dead," Thryimm interrupted flatly. "The machines will repair and maintain themselves if they are left alone long enough. It is the constant sabotage that causes the problem. Removing the Others removes the problem. There is no other way."

The Leader shook its head slowly. "No, I can't agree. You know I can't." It looked at Seeker and smiled sadly. "You can see the pass we're in. Can't even agree among ourselves. Well, but perhaps we're closer to a solution than we think, eh, Thryimm?"

"Perhaps," Thryimm admitted grudgingly.

"How so?" Seeker asked.

"Well, Thryimm has accomplished quite a coup, Questioner," the Leader said, beaming proudly at Thryimm. "You see, Thryimm has managed to capture the headman of the Others, their highest leader."

"This one knows everything we need to know to crush the rebellion of the Others thoroughly, once and for all," Thryimm said enthusiastically. "If we can get it to talk, this whole mess will soon be over."

"Ah," Seeker said mildly, "and this critical prisoner isn't talking, eh?"

"Well," Thryimm admitted slowly, "no, not yet. But soon, soon. The Prisoner will tell us what we need to know soon."

"Where are you keeping it?" Seeker asked.

"In a special dungeon in the abyss," Thryimm answered. "Well guarded and very secure."

"Why not in the city?"

The Leader and Thryimm both looked shocked. "Keep one of the Others in the city?" the Leader said. "Ah, ah, you don't understand, Questioner. They are creatures of the dark. They are hideous, deformed things that none of the Children of Light and Air could even look on without profound horror and disgust. To have one here in the city where it might be seen . . . Well, that is not even conceivable. A Vyinnlyirr seeing one of them would probably go mad with horror. No, no. We keep the Prisoner in the abyss, in a dungeon where no light ever shines and where no eyes can ever gaze fully on it. In utter darkness, Questioner. Utter darkness so not even those Vyinnlyirr that have to deal with it and question it will ever have to see it fully with all three eyes."

Seeker gave both Thryimm and the Leader a long, cold look. "You are 'questioning' the Prisoner? I assume that means you are torturing it for information?"

The Leader winced, but Thryimm's face remained expressionless. "Torturing it?" the Leader replied weakly. "Well, I hesitate to use such extreme terms, Questioner. We..."

"Yes," Thryimm interrupted harshly, "we are torturing it. We have tried all nonviolent means of gaining its cooperation we could think of. They yielded no results. Now we torture it. We have no choice."

"And you are getting the results you desired?" Seeker asked, its voice heavy with sarcasm.

"Well..." Thryimm hesitated, throwing an unreadable glance at the Leader. "Not exactly all we had hoped for..."

"In other words, nothing," Seeker suggested softly.

Thryimm paused, then nodded. "Nothing. It refuses to tell us anything. It simply says again and again that there are no more rebels, that the Others are all dead. It's lying, of course. The flickers continue, so there must still be rebels sabotaging the machines. That's as obvious as the beak on your face. But so far we haven't been able to break the Prisoner and force it to tell us where those rebels are hiding."

"Ah," Seeker said gently, a strange look fixed on its face, "so the Children of Light and Air are torturers."

"We have a mission," the Leader complained, "the Project, to fulfill. We certainly can't be expected to let anything stand in the way of that. We must..."

Thryimm was staring at Seeker, its face hard and cold. "Yes," it interrupted the Leader, "we are torturers. For the sake of the Project we are torturers. For the sake of the Project we would do even worse things."

"Like genocide?"

"Now, Questioner, please!" the Leader protested.

Thryimm paid no attention to the other Vyinnlyirr. "Yes. Like genocide. If the whole race of the Others must perish because they stand in the way of the Project, then they will perish. We destroyed this whole planet and almost every species on it for the Project, Questioner, so one more species won't stand in our way for very long."

Seeker turned to the Leader. "Is this why I was called? To resolve this issue?"

The Leader blinked, confused. "What issue?"

"The issue of the Others."

The two Vyinnlyirr exchanged surprised glances. Thryimm barked a harsh laugh and answered. "The fate of the Others is not an issue. It is already resolved. It is merely a matter of time, not one of decision."

"Then why was the Call sent out?"

"Ah, Questioner, Questioner, the Others are not the reason for the Call, no indeed! We certainly don't want you to give them another thought. They aren't worthy of it." The Leader had become positively jovial, although its tone rang hollow in Seeker's ears because the Novice noticed its hands were shaking. "And you really don't need to worry about the flickers, either. They are rare and not really important. Would you like the Keeper of Memories to give you more data on the early days of the founding of the city? There is some fascinating information on the building of the dome..."

"Can I meet with the Prisoner?" Seeker interrupted the inane flow of the Leader's monologue.

"Meet... meet..." the Leader stammered, unable even to complete the thought.

"Out of the question," Thryimm said sharply.

"Why?" Seeker demanded.

"Because even talking to one of the Others is enough to destabilize your host. Thassyil is not strong..."

"Thassyil," Seeker said softly, "survived the waste. Thassyil is not the same Vyinnlyirr you once selected as host *because* it was weak and foolish. We work together very effectively now, Thryimm."

I don't like the idea at all, Thassyil wailed in their shared mind. The abyss, the dark, those hideous things...

Don't worry, Thassyil, Seeker reassured the host, everything will be fine.

"We can't take that chance. More than one of my own Vyinnlyirr, who are specially trained, have become insane when in proximity to the Prisoner for more than a few moments. We conduct most of our conversations with the creature by remote now. It is simply too dangerous."

"Thryimm is right, Questioner. The waste is one thing. The abyss and the Others are another entirely. We can't risk losing our Questioner." The Leader's voice was appeasing but firm.

"So the abyss and the Prisoner are completely off limits for me?" Seeker asked calmly.

"That is correct," Thryimm affirmed coldly.

Seeker gave a huge sigh. "Well, then, I guess my mission here in the city is over. I can't think of anything else to question, and I have yet to discover why I was asked to come here. So there is no real reason to continue. I might as well..."

"Wait!" the Leader cried in panic. "No! Don't leave! No! Thryimm, can't we at least let the Questioner hear the sound recordings of the conversations you've had with the Prisoner? Isn't there some way to keep the Questioner happy? We can't let it go yet, we can't..."

Thryimm looked uncertain. "Well, I don't know. Going to visit the Prisoner in person is out of the question. But perhaps to hear the recordings... Will that do, Questioner?"

Seeker shrugged. "It will do for a start at least. Perhaps I will learn enough that way. Perhaps."

"Yes! Yes!" the Leader cried eagerly. "The recordings are just the thing! Please, Questioner, accept a chance to listen to the recordings!"

The Novice looked at the Leader, wondering why the creature was reacting so violently. The threat to leave the city was a strictly spur-of-the-moment ploy that had come to Seeker out of sheer frustration. Seeker had hardly expected it to work. If anything, Thryimm had looked positively relieved at the idea. But the suddenness and force of the Leader's response had thrown both Seeker and Thryimm off balance. The offer to listen to the recordings was hardly a solution to the real problem, but Seeker decided to follow up on it in hopes of drawing more out of the Leader's strange reaction. What was so important about having a Questioner here in the city? So far there didn't even seem to be a problem the Vyinnlyirr wanted any help with. But the Leader's panic at the thought that Seeker might leave was very real and undoubtedly significant. But what did it point to? More questions without answers, Seeker thought.

"When can I begin to listen to the recordings?" the Novice asked, for lack of anything better to say.

"Immediately!" the Leader announced with a look at Thryimm that urged acquiescence. "Right away!"

Thryimm glared sourly at the Leader, then at Seeker. "Not

for a few hours. I will have to find a place and collect the material. It is stored in a coded file. We don't want anyone to stumble over it by mistake and go insane hearing it. Why don't you go feed in your nest, Questioner, and I'll come for you in a while."

Seeker nodded, gave a farewell display to both the Leader and Thryimm, and then turned and left the hall at a calm pace.

"Must we listen to these conversations, Questioner?" Thassyil asked worriedly as they walked through the city back to their nest. "The very thought of the Others, real Others, frightens me."

"Stay hidden while I listen, then, if you like," Seeker said casually. "I won't need you."

The Novice could feel Thassyil bridle slightly at that. "Well, perhaps if I only listen halfway it won't be so bad," the Vyinnlyirr muttered. "After all, I did survive the waste.

"But once you hear the conversations, you'll be satisfied, won't you?" the host asked, a small suspicious note lurking in its question.

"Satisfied?" Seeker mused. "No, hardly. I'll listen to the conversations while we hunt for an opening to the abyss. I know they exist now. They must. Even though Thryimm claimed they were all sealed, there must still be a few, or else how could they have captured the Prisoner and occasionally go to question it?"

"Thryimm said it was questioned by remote," Thassyil protested weakly, dreading what it felt was coming.

"Thryimm said 'now' it was 'mostly' by remote. That implies there are still ways into the abyss."

"What . . . why do you want to get into the abyss?"

"Why else? To question the Prisoner directly!"

XVI.

Seeker shook its head and sighed. "Does this make any sense to you, Thassyil?"

The Vyinnlyirr's reply was hesitant. "Sense? Ummm, well, yes, it makes sense in a way, I suppose. I mean, it's just Thryimm asking the Prisoner questions."

"That's the point." The Novice's voice was heavy with a sense of frustration. "The questions. They are the same ones, over and over. There is no attempt to go beyond a very narrow focus. Leads and hints aren't followed up. Thryimm just pounds away at the same things again and again and again."

"Perhaps that's because the Prisoner never answers them," Thassyil suggested.

"But it does. I'll grant that the Prisoner's answers aren't always direct, but they all come down to the same thing: There aren't any more rebels. It is the last of them." Seeker paused thoughtfully. "It's almost as if Thryimm refuses to accept that answer and keeps endlessly asking until it gets the answer it wants. But that wouldn't make any sense. Why question someone if you don't want to hear the answer?"

Seeker paused as a new idea suddenly occurred to it. "Thassyil," it finally asked, "they couldn't be torturing the Prisoner just for fun, could they?"

"Fun?" Thassyil replied. "I don't understand the concept."

"Ummm. For the pleasure it gives them."

"Pleasure? From torturing another being? That's . . . that's unthinkable. How could one obtain pleasure from . . ." The Vyinnlyirr shuddered. "No. The answer to your question is no."

"But then why ask the same question over and over, not even changing the phrasing?"

"Because it's the question they want answered."

Seeker sighed. "You don't stand still when you kill a hornhead. You don't endlessly ask the same question in exactly the same way if you want an answer. It doesn't make sense. You have to come at it in different ways, from different angles, looking for an opening. It's like the unknown territory we talked about before. You walk around and around it until you get a sense for it. But to ask the same thing over and over, it just doesn't make sense . . . Unless," Seeker said thoughtfully, "Thryimm didn't really want an answer, or already knew it in advance."

"But that gets you back to the idea that Thryimm was torturing the prisoner just for pleasure."

"Or to the idea that the whole thing is a sham. When you think of it, Thassyil, the only proof we have that there even is a Prisoner is these tapes, which could be faked, and the word of Thryimm and the Leader. That's not a very substantial base of facts to work from."

"But why fake it? It seems like an awful lot of trouble to go to just to fool a Questioner. And why fool a Questioner in the first place? And what's more, how do you account for the flickers if the story is a fake?"

Seeker chuckled. "By my protoeggs, Thassyil, we'll make a Questioner out of you yet! All your points are valid. I can't answer a one of them. So there's only one thing to do."

"What's that?" Thassyil asked warily. "I don't like the sound of it, Questioner. The last time you said things like that, we ended up stumbling through the waste and I . . ." Thassyil paused as realization of what Seeker meant dawned on it. "You . . . you mean you want to go talk to the Prisoner yourself, don't you?" Its voice was soft with awe at the very idea. "You want to go into the dark abyss beneath the city, down where there is no light or air and talk to that hideous thing that lurks there, chained in the still darkness."

Seeker smiled. "Right. I can't think of anything else to do."

"I can," Thassyil said.

"What?"

"Let's go back into the waste and attack lizards. It's a lot more fun and not half so dangerous!"

They stood on the lowest level and stared about. "The problem," Seeker explained, "is worse than that of finding an exit to the waste. There we only had to cover the circumference of the circle the dome makes with the ground. Here we have the area of the same circle to deal with. The openings could be anywhere."

"But the Leader or Thryimm said they had all been sealed," Thassyil pointed out.

"Couldn't be true. At least one has to be open, or else Thryimm couldn't go to question the Prisoner. We'll just have to conduct a careful search, passage by passage."

"Well, at least it will take a good long time," Thassyil grumbled. "Personally, I hope it's in the last passageway we come to. I'm in no hurry to go into the abyss. The waste was enough adventure for one lifetime."

Seeker laughed. "At least there won't be any lizards in the abyss!"

"How do you know? Besides, even if there aren't any lizards, there could be something a lot worse. Those rebels could be there." Thassyil shuddered. "I don't even want to think what might happen if they found us."

"We'll worry about that when we find the opening. Let's get to it. This could take a while."

"The Questioner is searching for the opening to the abyss, Leader," Thryimm reported. "Even as you said it would."

"And Thassyil. How is Thassyil behaving?"

"It's hard to be sure, but I believe Thassyil is cooperating fully with the Questioner."

"Hmmmmm. Yes, it seems that way to me, too. Perhaps our choice of Thassyil as host was not a good one after all."

Thryimm shrugged. "Thassyil was a good choice at the time. But Thassyil has changed. It is no longer the foolish, vain Vyinnlyirr it was when we picked it."

"Yes, I suppose its experiences in the waste were bound to have some effect."

"It isn't just that, Leader. I get the feeling that Thassyil is actually working *with* the Questioner and doing so enthusiastically. If it opens itself up fully to its guest, it will give the Questioner resources we didn't intend it to have. And I don't merely mean Vyinnlyirr senses."

"But Thassyil's mind was blocked for all important information. And anyway, Thassyil was never involved with our special project. It can't reveal anything of real interest," the Leader said, but its tone held a note of uncertainty.

"True," Thryimm replied. "But there is still a lot of material in Thassyil's mind that I'd rather not have the Questioner aware of. And there's always the chance we overlooked something during the blocking. In any case, Thassyil's enthusiastic cooperation was not what we expected, and it may turn out to be dangerous."

The Leader nodded thoughtfully. "There's not much we can do but keep a close watch on them. Do you think they will find one of the entrances?"

Thryimm shrugged. "Eventually, yes."

"Do you think it might be a good idea to help them?"

"Perhaps. What do you have in mind?"

"Lissyi."

"Ah, the Blind One. Yes. A good idea. We can send Lissyi to them."

"Good. But let them search for a few days on their own. I don't want Lissyi to show up too suddenly. The Questioner might get suspicious."

They came around a corner onto a broad avenue and saw Lissyi shuffling toward them. Lissyi, Seeker said silently to Thassyil. How convenient.

Why do you say that? Thassyil asked. Are you suspicious of the Blind One?

Let's just say I'm suspicious of all coincidences now. Lissyi has managed to show up on several occasions in the past when I've been searching for something. It just seems too pat.

"Ah," Lissyi said as it approached them, "Questioner. What are you doing here?"

"Taking a stroll for health. I find it improves the digestion," Seeker replied. "What are you doing here?"

"I walk here often, here where the ruin of the city is most evident. It soothes me. Are you looking for something?"

"Why, yes. I'm looking for an entrance to the abyss," Seeker said bluntly.

Lissyi reared its head back, its beak opening in shock. "The ... the abyss? But why would you ..."

"Oh," Seeker said airily, "I enjoy visiting exotic and unusual places. You know, like the waste. Now that I've toured the waste and have seen the city, I'm ready for something new. And the abyss is about the only thing left on this planet I haven't seen." Seeker could feel Thassyil snickering.

"Ah," Lissyi said slyly, "a jest. Yes, of course, a jest. The Questioner wants to go into the abyss. It's not for Lissyi to ask why. No. Not for Lissyi."

"Well, do you know of any entrance?"

"Hmmmmm. Not as such. But there are some anomalies here and there in the walls that might be what you are looking for. I've noticed the anomalies, but I've never tried to find out what they are. I have no desire to visit the abyss." Lissyi shuddered.

"Well, then, can you show me these anomalies of yours?"

The Blind One cocked its head to one side as if listening. Then it nodded. " Yes, yes. Lissyi can show the Questioner. Come. Follow Lissyi." And the Blind One turned and began to amble off down the avenue.

Before long, the way began to narrow until finally they were in a twisting passage that was barely wide enough to walk down. Lissyi stopped at a point where the passageway made a sharp turn to the left and pointed to the blank wall. "There," the Blind One said, "is an anomaly."

Seeker stared hard at the wall, unable to see anything. Thassyil, it asked, can you help? Can you use your senses and translate for me?

Thassyil opened its third eye fully, closing the other two. Immediately a darker spot appeared on the wall. There, Thassyil said. See that place? The surface looks the same as the rest of the wall, but underneath, it's different.

Hollow? Seeker asked.

No, not hollow. But different. It might be ... I think there is a closing over an opening ... a ...

Door? Seeker suggested.

I don't know what a door is, but if it is something that closes off an opening, then that is what it is. A door.

"Lissyi," Seeker said softly, "how does one get to the anomaly? It seems to be behind the surface."

"Yes. Behind. Hmmmm. How does one get to it? I don't think one is supposed to. I think it is sealed permanently."

"Lissyi," the Novice said patiently, "do you know of any other anomalies, anomalies one could get to without having to blast a hole in the wall?"

Lissyi thought. "Perhaps one. Yes, perhaps. Shall we go to it? It is a long way from here."

"I have all the time in the city," Seeker replied with an ironic smile. "Let's go."

Once more the wall appeared normal to regular vision. It was the third eye that revealed the edges of an opening. Seeker checked it carefully. "Yes," the Novice said out loud. Then silently it spoke to Thassyil. It's like the opening to the waste that Thryimm took us through. Do you remember how he opened it?

Thassyil thought for a moment. Let me control the hands, it commanded Seeker. The Novice stepped back and let the Vyinnlyirr come to the fore. Muttering beneath its breath, Thassyil touched the wall in certain places. With a whoosh, the door opened inward.

Lissyi stepped back with alarm. "It's open! The way to the abyss is open! Are you . . . are you going in?"

Seeker peered into the darkness beyond the opening. "No," it said slowly, "not quite yet. I think we'll go back to the nest and get some food and the knives we used in the waste. Then we'll come back." Do you know of anything we can use for a light? Seeker asked its host.

Thassyil thought for a few moments. Perhaps we should ask Thryimm. It's most likely to have something. Of course it will become suspicious, but I imagine it knows we're looking.

Just not that we've found anything. Good. Let's do it.

Uh, Questioner, Thassyil said hesitantly, I, uh, suppose you're really serious about this, going into the abyss and finding the Prisoner?

Yes, Thassyil, I'm completely serious, Seeker said, unable to keep the amusement from its response. Does the prospect frighten or worry you?

Oh no, no, Thassyil replied glumly. I've always wanted to

go into the abyss. Really I have. Been my fondest dream for years. I love the dark.

Seeker chuckled. Well, the dark is really a good thing in this case.

How so?

Because then you can't see the rebels creeping up on us, and you can't see how hideous the Prisoner is. According to the Leader, the very sight would drive you mad.

Ah, yes, of course, Thassyil responded drily. I feel much, much better now, Questioner. You've really reassured me totally.

They both laughed.

"They're going in, then?" Thryimm inquired.

Lissyi shuddered. "Yes. Into the abyss. Is . . . is the Questioner insane or just foolish, Thryimm?"

"Perhaps both. It's hard to know with an alien species."

"And Thassyil?"

"Just insane."

Lissyi nodded. "Poor Thassyil. What will happen if they find the Prisoner?"

"Oh, they'll find it. Eventually. I really don't know what will happen. The Leader has never told me why it wants the Questioner to talk to the Prisoner. I don't know what will happen. But they will find it."

"Unless the rebels get them first," Lissyi said.

"Yes. Unless the rebels get them first."

They both laughed.

XVII.

Seeker paused before stepping through the entrance to the abyss. It checked the makeshift pack that was slung on its back, felt for the knives it carried at its waist, and flicked the light it held in its right hand on and off to make sure it worked properly. Then it squared its shoulders and prepared to step through the opening.

"Questioner," Thassyil muttered glumly before Seeker could take a step, "just promise one thing."

"All right, Thassyil," the Novice said, waiting patiently to give its host a chance to speak. "What do you want me to promise?"

"Well, I know how curious you are, always asking questions, always looking for answers. I understand why you want to talk to the Prisoner, although I don't understand what you hope to learn. But please promise that you'll question the Prisoner in the dark. Completely in the dark."

"Do you really believe what the Leader and Thryimm said about how hideous they are? That one look would drive a normal Vyinnlyirr insane?" Seeker's tone was skeptical.

"I don't know who or what to believe any more. But I don't want to take any chances. I didn't want to go out into the waste, and it turned out I had plenty of reasons for my fear."

"But we survived."

"Barely." Thassyil shuddered. "I don't want to come that close again, ever. What the Leader and Thryimm said may be a lie. The rebels and the Prisoner may be beautiful creatures, delightful to gaze on. But I don't want to take the chance. Please."

Seeker sighed. "All right, Thassyil. I promise. But we may have to use the light if the rebels attack us, you know. And then you'd have to see them."

"If the rebels attack I'll already be so frightened it won't make much difference! Look, I understand we'll have to use the light at times to find our way around the abyss, though most of the time I'd rather just use my third eye. I know it won't give a clear view of everything, but it should be good enough for finding our way around. And aside from that, the less I see of the abyss, the better. I just don't want to have to look at the Prisoner while you question it. Not with the light, not with my third eye, not with anything."

"That seems fair enough. I should be able to learn everything I want to know without having to look the creature in the face. Are you ready?"

Thassyil moaned softly. "As ready as I'll ever be. Let's go." With a last look around, Seeker stepped into the opening and into the abyss.

"They've entered." Thryimm turned from the display to address the Leader. "They're in the first level of the abyss."

"Ah, then the monitor works?"

"Perfectly. It's in the light I gave to the Questioner." Thryimm chuckled drily. "It was very cautious in asking for a light. Gave me a whole list of things, most of which were irrelevant, just to disguise the fact it wanted a light. I imagine it has no idea we know it is entering the abyss, much less that we want it to."

"I wouldn't be too sure of what the Questioner suspects and doesn't suspect. It seems to me we've underestimated its abilities from the very first." The Leader sighed with frustration. "It's so hard to deal with an alien mind."

"I still don't see why we needed a Questioner," Thryimm grumbled.

The Leader smiled smugly. "No, I don't expect you do. But we need it all the same. Perhaps you'll understand in the near future. Yes, perhaps once the Questioner has met and talked with the Prisoner, everything will become clear to you. In the meantime, keep a close watch on their movements and let me know how they are progressing on a regular basis."

Thryimm nodded morosely and turned back to the display, muttering beneath its breath.

"We've been here before," Thassyil declared. "I remember that queer blotch on the left."

"Hmmmm. I think you're right. We've gone in a circle for the last hour or so. No wonder, really, the way these damn tunnels twist and turn. Any ideas?"

Thassyil thought for a moment. "Last time I seem to remember we turned right at the next cross tunnel. Let's try left this time."

Seeker shrugged. "Sounds as good as anything. Let's give it a try. Concentrate on the turns we take, Thassyil. You seem to have a pretty good memory."

"Right," the Vyinnlyirr said with just a hint of pride.

They stopped at a place where three tunnels intersected and five choices of path were opened to them. For several moments they just stood there looking at the options.

"Questioner," Thassyil finally complained, "I'm hungry. The last time I mentioned that, you said we'd stop soon and eat. That was a long time ago."

Seeker chuckled. "All right. Let's stop here. We can think about which way to go while we eat." The Novice slung the sack from its back and squatted down next to a wall. Rummaging in the sack, it took out two handfuls of pellets and slowly ate them, savoring each one of them. "Won't be any lizards or snakes down here to eat, Thassyil," Seeker said. "We'll have to ration ourselves very carefully. Both food and water." Thassyil silently agreed.

"How long have we been wandering around down here?" Thassyil asked when they had finished eating and had washed the last mouthful down with a small sip of water.

"Well, I'm not really sure, but it seems we went at least one and a half feeding periods before eating. Might be two. I'm trying to stretch it out."

"Ummm," Thassyil mused, "so I've noticed. I think your species has something against eating, Questioner. You seem

City of Crystal Shadow 149

to..." Thassyil froze and whipped their head to the left. "What was that?" it whispered intently.

"What?" Seeker asked, trying to discern what had drawn the Vyinnlyirr's attention.

"I could swear I saw something move up that tunnel on the far left. Thought I heard it, too."

"I'll try the light," Seeker said, and turned on the light it held in its left hand. The sudden glare blinded them and for a moment made it impossible to see anything. But there was no mistaking the sudden sound of movement that came from several of the tunnels.

"There is something there!" Thassyil's voice held a quaver of raw fear. "It must be the rebels!"

"I don't think so," Seeker said reassuringly. "Sounded like some kind of small creature. Smaller than the lizards in the waste, in fact."

Thassyil pondered that. "I guess you're right. It didn't sound very big. But then, Thryimm never said how big the rebels are. Maybe..."

"No. I think more likely there is some small form of life that dwells in these tunnels. There were lizards and snakes and insects and arachnids in the waste. Why not something here? It makes sense."

"But what? And is it dangerous?"

Seeker chuckled. "I thought I was the Questioner! I don't know, Thassyil. But there's something here besides us. And besides the rebels and the Prisoner. We'll just have to keep our eyes and ears peeled. Whatever it is can doubtless see a lot better in the dark than we can, and that alone could make it dangerous."

"I knew I wasn't going to like this abyss business," Thassyil muttered. "Now we've got creatures as well as rebels. Might as well turn the light out. Whatever it was certainly isn't going to show itself in this much light."

"Right," Seeker replied, and switched off the light. For several moments, until their eyes adjusted back to the dark, they were blind. But there were no noises that indicated approaching monsters and soon they could see dimly again.

"Which tunnel?" Seeker asked.

Thassyil considered. "Well, the first movement was over that way. I don't like the idea one bit, but maybe we should go that way and see if we can find some sign of our visitor."

Seeker agreed and they set off again.

"Third level? My, they are progressing swiftly. The main machine level is only two more down. And then it's only two more to you know what." The Leader sat back and gazed thoughtfully at the display. "They seem to be doing quite well."

"It's that damn Thassyil, I'm sure of it," Thryimm accused. "Thassyil is cooperating fully now. Even suggesting things. I'm sure of it. There's no way the Questioner could use the third eye that way without help."

"Well, well, constantly new factors," the Leader mused. "But it seems to be going well. How long before . . . ?"

"Any time. They're in the right zone."

"Arachnids!" Seeker hissed and froze.

"Arachnids?" Thassyil wailed. "What in the name of the Project are arachnids doing down here? What could they eat? Aren't they all carnivores?"

"Not all. There are quite a few species that live on rotten vegetation. Some even eat live plants. There's one species I heard about that gets its nourishment directly from minerals in the ground. But, yes, most are carnivores. They eat any meat, including each other. They're damn dangerous when they're solitary types, but there are several social species that are some of the most frightening creatures in the universe."

"What are these?" Thassyil asked, its voice quivering with fright.

"I only caught a quick glimpse through your third eye. Can you play it back from memory? Ah, good. Hmmmmm. Slightly smaller than the lizards in the waste. About two feet across. Hmmmm. Doesn't look good, Thassyil. Looks like a hunting arachnid. See how the legs are long and built for speed? Looks like the thing could jump a good distance, too. And I think it has fangs. Damn." Seeker took out both of its knives. "We'd best go slow and easy from here on. If you kept a sharp watch before, double it!"

It was Seeker who first realized something was behind them, following cautiously, stopping when they stopped, moving when they moved. Only once did it move after they halted, and that one time Seeker heard it. "We're being stalked," it announced to Thassyil.

"Arachnid?" the Vyinnlyirr mumbled, almost unstrung with fear.

"I think so." Seeker tried to sound calm. It didn't want its host to panic. "Thassyil," it said, "please, Thassyil, don't run out on me. I need you now, more even than in the waste. Your senses are critical for our survival. I know you hate the abyss and that the arachnids frighten you. But I can't afford to be without you. I can't lock you off into your own hidey-hole now. I *need* you."

Thassyil was silent for a long moment and Seeker could feel the Vyinnlyirr trying to pull itself together. Finally it spoke, its voice calmer. "I understand. You need me. I'll . . . I'll do my best. But I'm very scared, Questioner."

"Me, too, Thassyil. I think arachnids scare me more than any other lifeform in the universe. There was one on Labyrinth that . . . oh, why talk about that! Let's go."

They moved carefully, checking behind and ahead before every step. Both knives were out and ready to throw.

In a short time, they came to a place where their tunnel entered a small domelike space perhaps fifteen feet across. Two other passageways led out of the space. Seeker hesitated at the mouth of the tunnel it occupied, looking carefully into the open area and checking out the mouths of the other tunnels. Everything seemed quiet; even the stalker behind it was utterly silent.

Hesitantly, unsure, Seeker stepped into the open and began to cross it toward the left-hand tunnel. Halfway across it heard a flurry of motion. In the mouths of the two tunnels, arachnids appeared. The Novice half turned to go back into the tunnel it had left. The arachnid that had been stalking it was crouched there.

Slowly, trying to watch all three arachnids at the same time, Seeker backed against the nearest wall. "Calm, Thassyil," it pleaded, "calm."

"I'm . . . I'm doing the best I can," came the strangled, quavering reply. "What . . . what about the light?"

"The light?" Seeker asked, only half paying attention to the Vyinnlyirr. "What do you mean?"

"I mean . . ."

Suddenly the three arachnids chittered and sprang as one at Seeker. The Novice hurled the knife in its left hand, but Thassyil had dropped the one in the right and grabbed the light, which was attached to the belt. The Vyinnlyirr closed all three of its eyes tightly and turned the light on, then threw itself to the floor, rolled and leapt to its feet. It switched the light off and opened its eyes.

Everything had happened so suddenly that Seeker had been unaware it had lost control until it opened its eyes again. It saw that one of the arachnids was down and dying, the knife deep in its head area. The other two were dazed and staggering in reaction to the sudden flash of light. Realizing this was its only chance, Seeker picked up the knife Thassyil had dropped and stepped swiftly to the two arachnids, slashing them quickly and deeply. They screamed horribly and died.

Panting, shaking violently in a sudden reaction, Seeker stepped back and almost collapsed against the wall of the open area. "They're social, Thassyil, social arachnids. They were hunting us together in a pack. They communicated just before they attacked. They . . . Thassyil! If you hadn't thought of the light we wouldn't have had a hope! Thassyil! Thassyil!"

Seeker realized that its host was unconscious. The Novice chuckled shakily, stepped away from the wall and went over to collect its other knife. "Damn, Thassyil," it said out loud, "we are turning out to be one tough team!"

XVIII.

Seeker stood and gazed about in awe. Crystalline light filled the air with subtle, shimmering colors that flowed and swirled, combining and separating and then coming together again in new mixes that teased and stunned the eye. The roof of the huge cavern glowed and pulsed with a vast rainbow of hues, while the distant walls glowed softly, changing shades almost faster than the mind could follow.

But the true wonders were the huge crystals that lay scattered almost haphazardly about the floor of the cavern. They towered over the Novice, each facet coruscating with a play of intense color. Light rippled across their surfaces and now and then flashed suddenly to blind the eye with glory.

The floor and the very air itself pulsed with an urgent, beating vibration that went to the very core of Seeker's being, making its whole body beat in trembling sympathy. There were rhythms in the vibrations, complex, beautiful, demanding, right. Seeker could not help but respond to them.

For many minutes the Novice could only stand and gaze at the wonder that filled its eyes. Then it sighed and whispered in a reverent tone, "It was all worth it, the waste, the hunger, the thirst, the dark, the spiders, all worth it, just to see this. This is the heart of your city, Thassyil, the soul. And it is even more incredibly beautiful than what lies above."

Seeker could tell that Thassyil was just as impressed as it was. "I . . . I never knew it was like this down here. I've never been here, never heard of anyone who has been. It was never even talked about. It's . . . it's incredible! This is the machinery that keeps the city running, that provides light and food and air and water and everything else the Vyinnlyirr need. That's an awesome idea by itself, but to think it looks like this . . ." Its voice trailed off in wonder.

"Your race, or at least those ancestors who built this, must have been one of the greatest in the universe, Thassyil," Seeker said solemnly. "I've never heard or read of anything remotely like this anywhere."

"Yes," Thassyil muttered in reply, "yes, once we must have been very great." It paused and then continued, a bitter edge entering its thought. "But now we are much, much less. We couldn't even repair these wondrous machines, much less create new ones. And someday even they will cease working and the city will fall utterly into ruins. The wind and sand will slowly wear it away until this glory is but a pitiful nub. Where will our greatness be then, Questioner?"

Seeker was silent for several moments. When it finally spoke, its tone was soft and musing. "Remember in the waste, Thassyil, when we looked up at night and saw those cold, heartless, eternal stars looking back at us with relentless, unconcerned stares? I know that I cursed them then, cursed their eternalness and indifference. But now I know I was wrong. For the stars aren't eternal, Thassyil. They are born, live, and then die. It takes them much longer than it takes me, at least in terms of my sense of time. But who can say how they feel? Perhaps they weep bitterly over their doom and helplessly curse the inevitable entropic fate that awaits them. They may see their life spans as fleeting, all too short episodes in a universe that seems eternal by comparison.

"I remember on my home world there was a plant, with a very beautiful and delicate blossom of intense crimson color. There was a time of every year named for this plant, the Season of Red Beauty. It was the shortest of all our seasons, for these plants grew in one day, blossomed the next, and died and shriveled the third.

"I recall how I waited for them every year, watching impatiently until their tender shoots appeared. The day the blossoms opened, I would just wander about, breathing in their fragrance, filling my eyes with their wonder. And then they would wither and die and I felt empty and angry and helpless. And strangely abandoned.

"I often wondered, at times like that, if those flowers didn't envy me. I saw their generations come and go. Did they see me wandering through their multitudes and bemoan their own temporality as against my seeming immortality? Just the same way I cursed the stars out on the waste?

"Did you know, Thassyil, there are worlds out there in the universe, worlds dead now, but where life once flourished? And some of them have been dead for ten million years? We don't even know what some of those beings looked like, much less what they felt or thought. I wonder, did they ache because they knew that some day they would be gone and that all trace, all memory of them would vanish from existence? And there are holes in space, Thassyil, holes where once whole star systems existed, gone now, utterly, utterly gone. Not even light comes out of them any more. Did those systems, or the creatures that lived in them, look out at the universe and hurl bitter curses into the dark because they felt their imploding fate approaching, because they felt their own mortality?" Seeker fell silent.

"Is that why you became a Questioner? Because you feared your own mortality?" Thassyil asked gently. "Did you want to save a whole world and live forever through them?"

Seeker gazed silently at the play of colors that swirled through the air of the cavern. "Fear my own mortality? Yes, I suppose I do. I guess I want to be immortal, to live forever. But it's not possible, for if even the stars die, what hope has a foolish Questioner?"

"But a Questioner that saves a whole world ... surely such a one lives on in the memory of those saved!"

The Novice barked a harsh laugh. "Memory! Ha, that's a thin way to exist, Thassyil! And the odds are they would eventually forget or get it all wrong, or ... No, I have no hope of immortality any longer. At least not of the kind I may once have hungered after. I ... I'm not too sure what I hope for now.

"But I do know one thing, one thing I've realized just while standing here and seeing all this dying beauty. I am one with the stars and this city and the crimson flowers and all those dead and gone worlds. One. For I, too, am mortal." Seeker paused and laughed silently. "Not much to share in, eh? But at least it's real!

"This"—Seeker gestured widely at the cavern and its crystal machines—"all this needs a lot of time to be thought about and digested. I know there is something significant here for me, if I can only work my way through to it. Perhaps after this mission is over, when I'm in stasis, my mind will worry it into meaning. Perhaps. And then again, perhaps it will always remain a gaping hole of doubt right in the middle of my mind, my own personal abyss."

Thassyil simply stayed silent. There seemed to be nothing it could say. Indeed, it realized, it would have to deal with exactly the same personal abyss.

The two of them stood and gazed around for a good hour. Then with a shrug, Seeker began to plod determinedly around the edge of the vast cavern, looking for another exit.

"Two more levels, Leader," Thryimm said nervously. "And then they reach . . ."

"I know, I know," the Leader interrupted. "I think it very likely they will succeed, don't you?"

"But can we allow it?"

"Do we really have any choice?"

"But why do we need a Questioner? Why not simply destroy it before it finds out? The only thing we really lose is Thassyil, and that's no loss at all. Someone else can take up its duties on the Project and . . ."

"But who, then, will take up the Questioner's duties on the Project?" the Leader asked softly.

Thryimm seemed stunned and confused. "The Questioner's duties? The Questioner has no duties on the Project! It is an alien! It can't have any . . ."

The Leader smiled mysteriously. "You know only what you know, Thryimm. I know what I know. I know the Questioner has a role to play. Let that be enough for you. You have no need to know more.

"We will allow them to proceed. If they succeed, wonderful. If not, well, there are alternative plans, to be sure.

"Carry on, Thryimm. Watch their progress closely. Let me know when they arrive at their destination." The Leader turned and left without another word.

Thryimm, still looking stunned, nodded dumbly.

* * *

"Questioner," Thassyil whispered, "something is wrong with this tunnel."

Seeker stopped dead in its tracks. "Wrong? What do you mean? Do you sense the arachnids again?"

"No," Thassyil said, its tone uncertain. "It's not that. It's something about the tunnel itself. There's a sense of danger here, but not of the arachnids. It's more... more the tunnel itself, as if it... Perhaps you should turn on the light so we can see more clearly."

Seeker nodded and turned on the light. The Novice gasped with surprise. About two feet in front of it, the floor of the tunnel simply disappeared for about five feet. "By my protoeggs," Seeker whispered, "there's something wrong all right! If we'd taken just two more steps...!"

Thassyil cringed at the thought. "How do we get across? Or do we even want to get across?"

"We want to, all right. Thassyil, this can only mean we're getting closer! This is probably just as much to keep the Prisoner in as to keep us out!"

"Perhaps," Thassyil replied uncertainly, "but how do we get across it?"

"We jump," Seeker said simply.

"Jump?" Thassyil asked nervously. "Jump across that... that... How far down do you think it goes?"

"Far enough," Seeker shrugged. "If you'd rather think of it as soaring or gliding instead of jumping, that's all right by me. But that's the only way across that I can see. So that's the way we go!"

"Gliding," Thassyil muttered. "We were a lot smaller and our membranes a lot larger when we used to glide. But maybe gliding is the way to think of it. We'll go back a few paces, counting every step, then turn and run hard, again counting every step. Then we'll fling ourselves into the air and spread our membranes and glide over that chasm and... Questioner, I don't like this one bit!"

"Me either. Ready?" Seeker asked calmly.

"Ready," Thassyil replied with a quaver in its voice.

They ran hard and jumped. For an instant, leaping in the dark, they were both sure they had jumped short and would fall endlessly into the empty chasm. But then their feet hit the passage floor with a solid jolt. They staggered to their knees and then wobbled upright.

For several moments neither of them could speak. Finally Thassyil managed to squeak out, "Let's keep the light on from here on out, eh?"

"Yes," Seeker agreed, its heart still beating furiously. "Sounds like a good idea. Might be more of these, or even worse."

There was worse. A crystal that shot out a beam of intense red light and barely missed decapitating them. A part of the floor that tilted and nearly dropped them into another abyss. A section of the wall that collapsed and almost crushed them.

But with each trap, they became more and more certain they were on the right path, the path that led to the Prisoner.

"Remember your promise," Thassyil said again and again. "No light of any kind when we talk to the Prisoner. I'm on the point of collapse with all these traps. Seeing that monster face to face would be enough to push me over the edge."

Seeker snorted. "I think you're underestimating yourself, Thassyil, and overestimating the hideousness of the Prisoner. But if that's what you want, I agree. I promised, and I'll try to stick to it as best I can."

"I don't like the tone of that," Thassyil said with sudden suspicion. "It sounds like you're playing games with words there, Questioner. What are you saying?"

Seeker sighed. "All right, all right. Have it your way. No light of any kind."

"They are almost there, Leader," Thryimm reported. "When I left the monitor, they were perhaps two hundred yards from the Prisoner's cell."

"They'll find the cell?"

"The corridor they are in ends at the door to the cell."

"Ah," the Leader smiled, "even Thassyil can't miss that one. Good, good. Now, if the Questioner will only do as I expect it to . . ."

"I'm certain it will question the Prisoner. I will record every word spoken. Perhaps the Questioner will be able to learn something we have failed . . ."

The Leader waved its hand in dismissal. "No, that's not what I meant. Of course the Questioner will question the Prisoner. But that's not what I meant. Record it if you wish. I doubt we will learn anything new. I suspect the Prisoner has told us all it knows and all that really matters. Thank you for your report, Thryimm," the Leader said in dismissal. "Let us hope all goes well now."

The corridor ended in a door. They moved cautiously to the door and listened intently in an attempt to ascertain what might lie on the other side. A soft rustling came to them, and then a low moan of something in pain.

"What do you think?" Seeker questioned.

"I think we can't go any further and this must be it."

"Sounds like there's something behind the door."

"The Prisoner?"

"I hope so. If it's the rebels . . ."

"Turn off the light," Thassyil hissed. "The only thing to do is open the door and see. Turn off the light. When we open the door, I'll give a quick look with my third eye. I should be able to see vague outlines, even in this dark. That way I'll know if it's just one creature or more. If it's more, turn on the light to stun them. We'll keep all three eyes shut tight like we did with the arachnids."

"All right," Seeker whispered in reply. "Get ready now. Wait. Let me take one of the knives out. Right. All right. I'm turning out the light. Now, on the count of three, I'll give the door a shove and we'll step in."

"What if it doesn't open?"

"There isn't any kind of lock or even a latch that I can see. It should open. If it doesn't, well, we'll try something else. One, two, three!"

They pushed the door with all their strength and it flew open with a resounding crash. They almost tumbled into the room. They quickly regained their balance and Thassyil swept the tiny cell with its third eye. Over in the corner, not more than ten feet away, a single form huddled on the floor.

"Come in, come in," a deep voice rasped to them out of the darkness. "Close the door and come in. Since you're not Thryimm, you're welcome. Sorry I can't come to greet you, but I'm chained to the wall, you see."

XIX.

"Ah, ah, I would say it is good to see you, but of course that would be foolish of me since I can't see you any better than you can see me," the Prisoner said.

"You can't see us?" Seeker asked, surprised. "Why, I would think your race would be adapted to seeing here in the abyss. How do you get around?"

"Ha! Well, you see, it hasn't always been dark here in the abyss. Once the place was ablaze with light. Every passage, every chamber was filled with brightness. But then they shut it all off from up above someplace. Yes, they plunged us into darkness when the 'rebellion' broke out."

Seeker stood near the door of the cell. Over against the opposite wall it could make out a vague form. Since the voice came from that direction, the Novice assumed that must be where the Prisoner was, chained to the wall. Thassyil reminded Seeker once again that it had promised not to turn the light on and then retired sulkily to its own corner of the mind they shared.

"So you've only had to live in the dark recently, then?" Seeker asked.

"Recently? Hmmmmm, recently. No, longer than recently, I fear. You see, the so-called rebellion broke out about thirty-five hundred years ago and the lights went out five hundred years later. So it's been dark now for three thousand years, give or take a few hundred."

"Three thousand?" Seeker was stunned. "But... but the Leader gave no indication the rebellion had been going on for so long. I just assumed that..."

The Prisoner laughed harshly. "Ah, yes, the Leader. And Thryimm, no doubt! Oh, they'll let you assume all sorts of things. But here in the abyss we assume nothing! Precisely who are you and what do you want with me?"

"I apologize. There is no way you could know who or what I am. I am a Questioner, called here by the Leader. I discovered that you existed here in the abyss and wanted to talk with you."

"A Questioner? Called by the Leader? Why?"

"That," Seeker said drily, "is the one question I can't seem to find any answer to."

The Prisoner chuckled. "And so you came down here to see if I knew? A strange idea."

"No," Seeker said slowly, "that's not why I came here. There are many things on this planet which just don't seem to fit together into a sensible pattern. The rebels in the abyss and their leader, the Prisoner, was one of the pieces that made no sense. So I decided to come talk to you myself and see if I could make anything out of it."

"Hmmmmm," the Prisoner mused in the darkness. Seeker could sense, rather than see, it shift its position slightly. The faint clank of a chain came to the Novice's ears. "And of course you have been told we rebelled because we wanted to come up into the city, even to return to the surface of the planet. And that when they refused to allow this, we began to sabotage the machines that keep the city running."

"Well, yes," Seeker answered hesitantly.

"And that they fought a long battle against us. And that I was the leader of the rebellion and had been captured and kept a prisoner here while they tried to extract information from me about the whereabouts of the rest of the rebel force." The Prisoner stopped abruptly with a laugh. "Rubbish like that, eh?"

"Yes," Seeker replied, uncertain what else to say.

"Well, then, you already know everything, so why come down here into the abyss and question me?"

Seeker hesitated for a moment before speaking. "Because I

don't know how much of what the Leader says is true or accurate. I'd rather find out myself whenever possible. I went out into the waste in search of the Others and instead found Vyinnlyirr living in tunnels. Now I have been told that the Others are actually here in the abyss and I wanted to find out if this was any truer than what I had been told about the waste."

"Into the waste?" the Prisoner said with surprise. "My, my, you are an adventurous one! And you found nothing but Vyinnlyirr? How interesting. What do you expect to find here?"

"The rebels. Or at least their leader."

"And why should the rebels reveal themselves to you and talk with you? You come in the body of one of the city Vyinnlyirr. Why should the rebels, the Others, trust you any more than they trust Thryimm or the Leader?"

"Because," Seeker protested, "I am a Questioner, and . . ."

The Prisoner laughed raucously. "What do we know or care about Questioners here in the abyss? We did not call you. You mean nothing to us. Why should we cooperate? Nothing good will come of it for us. You are the Leader's idea, the Leader's creature, not ours. Go away. You disturb my rest. I need to gather strength for my next questioning. Thryimm is not gentle." The Prisoner fell silent.

Seeker stood for a moment, undecided as to what to do. It felt Thassyil stir in its mind. We came a long way for a greeting like this, Questioner, Thassyil said. I don't think we should leave until we have some better answers than that. I agree, Seeker replied. Then the Novice spoke out loud to the Prisoner. "Are you actually the leader of the rebels?"

The Prisoner sighed. "The leader? It seems to me the idea of a leader implies a following. And I have none. Therefore, how can I be a leader?"

"You have no following?"

The Prisoner laughed bitterly. "I've told Thryimm this same thing a thousand times. There are no rebels. They are all dead. I am the last survivor. I am the leader and the followers all wrapped up into one."

"But the flickers continue. I've seen them. So someone must still be sabotaging the machines."

The Prisoner snorted. "On your way here you passed the level where the machines are. Did you see any signs of sabotage? Or for that matter, did you see anything that might even be sabotaged? Think of those vast crystals you saw humming and glowing. What would you have done to them to make them break down?"

"Well," Seeker said uncertainly, "I don't know much about the technology..."

"No more and no less than we do!" the Prisoner crowed. "Don't you see, Questioner? We know as little of how to fix or break the machines as those in the city above do! Or as you do! That kind of knowledge died thousands of years ago. We are as helpless to sabotage the machines as the Leader is to fix them!"

"Then what causes the flickers?"

"How should I know?" the Prisoner replied. "Perhaps the machines are simply breaking down after thousands of years of operation. But I can assure you the flickers are not the result of sabotage carried out by me or any rebels!"

"Then what about the rebellion?" Seeker heard itself say, realizing even as it spoke that it was Thassyil asking the question.

"The rebellion never existed," the Prisoner answered bitterly. "Oh, it's true that those of us in the abyss wished to leave it for the city or the surface. But we never rebelled, never destroyed any machines, never harmed any of those in the city. We simply asked to leave. And then asked again and again and again until they shut off the lights. That's your rebellion!"

"But why would they act that way toward you?" Seeker asked in confusion. Because, Thassyil answered, they are the Others! They are hideous creatures! We couldn't have them wandering the streets of the city, or even the waste!

"Because," the Prisoner said in a hissing voice, "we refused to participate in their damn fool Project! Because we threaten the very foundation it is based on, the very idea..."

"The Project?" Seeker interrupted. "How could you threaten the Project?"

"The Project!" the Prisoner laughed sharply. "The beloved Project! The whole purpose for the city, the life and soul of the Children of Light and Air! A farce, a foolishness, an idiocy!

"What is this glorious Project, Questioner? The Vyinnlyirr investigating the Vyinnlyirr! Nonsense! Tell me, how does the hammer hammer itself? Any attempt to study oneself results in one studying oneself studying oneself. The act changes the very nature of the thing being studied. Rather than an object under observation, it becomes the subject observing itself observing.

"But what is truly subject and what object? What type of relationship could exist between a subject studying an object that was the subject itself and the object being studied which was really the subject doing the studying? There is a circle here that cannot be broken out of. You can't pull yourself from the mud by grabbing your own head and lifting.

"That kind of a circle leads to an endless inward spiraling, a sure descent into insanity. The study becomes more important than life itself. The whole city, every aspect of Vyinnlyirr life is dedicated to the Project. And what does the Project do? Study every aspect of Vyinnlyirr life. Which is dedicated to the Project. Which studies every aspect of Vyinnlyirr life which is dedicated to the study of every aspect of Vyinnlyirr life. Every normal instinct, every normal drive is twisted into the spiral and turns back on itself like a serpent biting its own tail.

"And once that serpent has bitten and taken hold, it begins to eat. Yes, the Project eats itself and the Vyinnlyirr with it! It is insanity! Life that is not part of the Project becomes irrelevant and eventually hateful and something to be destroyed. Life that is part of the Project becomes lifeless since it is the Project studying the Project.

"And what is it all based on? This whole great Crystal City, this magnificent monument to futility has as its foundation the belief that somehow the Vyinnlyirr mind can know itself. This assumption is treated as though it were a fact! But is it a fact?" The Prisoner chuckled darkly. "A fact! There are no facts. Only interpretations. I'm not saying that knowledge is purely subjective, because even that would merely be an interpretation that attempts to impose its own version of reality. All I'm pointing out is what the Leader and Thryimm and others like them refuse to notice: that they have founded themselves not on fact, but on interpretation. And what is that interpretation itself based on? A need, a desire, a lust to compel all things to follow a certain form. But that form is only one among many, and any attempt to force all into its shape is stupid and untrue!

"How can the Project learn everything there is to know about the Vyinnlyirr? That could only be accomplished from outside the race, if it is possible at all, and only from several points of view. How would any evaluation be conceivable without some standard to measure against? Yet the Vyinnlyirr isolate themselves and have nothing to compare themselves with. They have destroyed all but a few minor lifeforms on this planet. Where is the comparison to come from? Oh, and there is an even bigger question, one that would cause the whole city to come crashing down if it were even asked! Yes, Questioner, it is all insanity!"

The Prisoner laughed wildly. "Insanity, Questioner! That is what the City of Light and Air is based on! That is its foundation! The Vyinnlyirr see their Project as a straight line leading from the past into the future. At one end, sixty thousand years ago, is the question, the thing that started it all in motion. At the other end, somewhere out there in the future, is the answer." The Prisoner's voice was shouting and almost hysterical. "But they fail to see that the line is not straight! It is a vast circle! A snake biting its own tail and eating as fast as it can! Insanity!"

The Prisoner stopped for a moment. Seeker stood tensely, not sure what to expect next. Its mind was awhirl with speculation. The Novice could feel Thassyil reeling under the impact of the Prisoner's accusations.

Suddenly Seeker heard a new noise in the cell, a sound it had never heard in the city or in the waste. At first it could not identify the sound. Then it realized it was the sound of sobbing. The Prisoner was weeping!

"And what . . . is the result?" the Prisoner managed to get out between the deep sobs that were racking its body. "The native species on this planet have been all but destroyed. The planet itself was raped and used up to build the city. The Others were enslaved and finally exterminated. And those left to dwell in the city, chained to the Project, have become mere shadows of true life, endlessly circling around and around and around." The Prisoner's voice rose to a sudden shriek. "And I am kept here, chained away from the light, so they can torture me and ask me questions about a rebellion that never existed!" The sobbing became uncontrollable.

Seeker sagged against the wall, almost overwhelmed by the Prisoner's words. Thassyil was floundering badly, confused and frightened. For a moment or so, Seeker drifted, unable to think clearly or decide what to do. Then, suddenly, it knew what it had to do.

Thassyil, it warned its host silently, hide as deeply as you can. I have to do something I promised not to do. I have to turn on the light. I must see the Prisoner face to face.

NO! Thassyil screamed inwardly. No! Don't turn on the light, Questioner! Don't! There's no place to hide. I . . . I'm not sure I can stand it! It's all so confusing! Please, you promised!

I'm sorry, Seeker replied harshly. I must. Brace yourself.

Seeker turned the light on. The Prisoner gasped in surprise and Thassyil wailed in fright. For the moment, though, the light was so sudden, and it had been so dark for so long, that Seeker was blinded and could see nothing.

Then its eyes adjusted and it stared across the cell at the creature that was chained to the wall. With a piercing scream, Thassyil collapsed and the shock sent Seeker stumbling for the door. The light fell from its hand and tumbled to the floor, filling the cell with brightness. The Novice smashed into the wall, gasping for breath. Behind it, it heard the Prisoner laughing insanely, shrieking, and crying all at the same time.

Bracing itself against the wall next to the door, Seeker turned back to look at the Prisoner one more time to make sure it had actually seen what it thought it had.

There, huddled against the wall, staring blindly into the glare of the unexpected light, was an ancient Vyinnlyirr!

XX.

"Vyinnlyirr! They're all Vyinnlyirr!" the Novice shouted at the Leader. "There are no Others. Not in the waste, not in the abyss. Nowhere."

The Leader nodded slowly. "Yes. Vyinnlyirr."

"There never were any Others, were there?" Seeker said more calmly. "The whole thing with the Keeper of Memories. It was all a fraud. There never was another home world with a double star. It was an elaborate hoax, an attempt to put me off the truth."

"You are correct," the Leader admitted with a quiet smile. "There never was another home world. This is where we have been forever. We've never developed any sort of star-drive, never even tried to. Travel of that sort doesn't interest us."

"But why all the lies?" Seeker asked.

"Because you had to see things through your own eyes. We wanted you to find the Vyinnlyirr of the waste and of the abyss on your own, to discover and study them without any preconceptions. It had to be a surprise."

"But why did I have to find them? Why no preconceptions? What does it all have to do with the Call?"

The Leader studied Seeker for a moment as if trying to decide precisely how to proceed. Finally it said, "You have seen the

Vyinnlyirr from three very different vantage points. First, you came to know the Vyinnlyirr of the city, the finest, highest, example of the Children of Light and Air, deeply and profoundly involved in the Project. Then you met the Vyinnlyirr of the waste, a primitive race, in its natural state, struggling directly with nature, virtually unaware of the Project. Finally, you encountered the Prisoner, dweller in the dark, false world of the abyss, a degenerate rebel against the Project. No other creature has ever had such an opportunity. To experience the Vyinnlyirr from three such totally disparate perspectives.

"You now have a unique viewpoint, Questioner, one not available to anyone else in our long history. One we could not duplicate no matter how hard we tried. Any perspective we attempted would always come from the same place. Yours and yours alone is unique."

Seeker threw up its hands in exasperation. "You planned for all this to happen? For the journey into the waste? For the trip into the abyss? For the nearness of death on so many occasions? This was all what you wanted to happen?"

"Yes," the Leader declared briefly.

"But Thassyil and I could have died numerous times. We came very close on several occasions, at least three times in the waste and once in the abyss. And now, with the seeing of the Prisoner, I think Thassyil may have gone insane. I can't get it to come out of the corner it is hiding in. All it does is wail in fear. Did you plan that, too?"

The Leader sighed resignedly. "Certain risks could not be avoided. That was one of the reasons we needed a Questioner. Any creature, we thought, that could survive Labyrinth could survive this trial. It seems we were correct. It is regrettable if we lost Thassyil in the process."

"But why? What was the point to it all? You've never been willing to tell me why you wanted a Questioner in the first place."

The Leader smiled slightly. "The Prisoner referred to it at one point, but never expanded on it. I imagine the creature felt that what it was referring to was a fatal flaw in the Project. But it was wrong, they were all wrong, those who fought the Project and refused to understand it!"

"What are you talking about? The Prisoner said many things ...Wait...it did indicate there was a bigger question, one that could cause the downfall of the whole city if it was even asked. Is that what you're referring to?"

"Yes," the Leader nodded solemnly. "Yes, that's it. Only the Prisoner is wrong. It is not the downfall of the city or the Project, but rather its very salvation!" The Leader began to pace back and forth, its head bobbing in time with its words. "You see, Questioner, the Project is an exhaustive exploration of every aspect of the Vyinnlyirr, the complete explication of a sentient race. Nothing even approaching it has even been attempted before! It is the greatest intellectual endeavor of all time!

"But a race cannot be finally evaluated until it is dead and gone. The story is not finished until the words 'the end' are spoken. For as long as the Vyinnlyirr still exist, things can change, and constantly new material must be added to the study. The prospect is endless... unless the Vyinnlyirr reaches its own end!"

The Leader whirled suddenly and fixed Seeker with an intense stare. "You see, Questioner, the Vyinnlyirr of the city, of the waste, and of the abyss are experiments. Three different forms of the same species. They were all necessary to explore the possibilities of the species as fully as could be done. And there have been other experiments in our long history, I assure you."

"Experiments?" Seeker asked, a bitter taste in its mouth. "You consider yourselves and those other Vyinnlyirr merely experiments? Thassyil, Syssir, Thryimm, all just experiments?"

"Yes!" the Leader hissed. "Yes, nothing more, nothing less. The Project, Questioner, that is the real thing! All the rest doesn't count! The Vyinnlyirr are merely things to be studied, things..."

Seeker looked at the Leader in horror. "But you are a Vyinnlyirr! How can you talk about your own species as if they were mere experimental animals? How can you..."

"Because that's all they are!" the Leader shouted. "I am no Vyinnlyirr, Questioner! There is no reality to the Vyinnlyirr! We are just the way the Project works itself out. I am an aspect of the Project. The Project is the only true reality!"

It's... it's insane, Seeker heard from a corner of its mind. Thassyil! the Novice cried with relief. Are you all right? You've given me quite a fright. I couldn't reach you and...

The Leader, Thassyil continued coming more and more from its corner. It's insane, Questioner! What it's saying is crazy!

Seeker looked up at the Leader. The Vyinnlyirr was staring at it, its eyes wide and bright, its hands like claws, its expression intent to the point of mania.

"What do you want from me, Leader?" Seeker asked. "What do you want a Questioner for?"

"To write the last chapter! To close the book on the Vyinnlyirr! To complete the Project! Surely you see it all now, Questioner! We cannot do it ourselves. If even one of us survived, the Project would not be complete because that one Vyinnlyirr would not be finally analyzed. No. We must come to an end, and then the last data must be fed into the Project by someone not of the Vyinnlyirr. You, Questioner!"

"You're insane!" Seeker felt itself saying. But it was Thassyil who was speaking. Thassyil had recovered fully and had actually stepped in front of Seeker to take over the mind. "You're planning the death of all the Vyinnlyirr!"

"Yes!" the Leader cried. "But not I. No, no, not I. I plan and execute nothing. I am a mere cog in the Project. It is the Project which has planned it all, the Project which has worked out every detail and needed only one last thing, this Questioner, to consummate the plan it had been working on for thousands of years. All the Vyinnlyirr, all dead with one master stroke! A simple virus, deadly, incurable, totally effective! Every Vyinnlyirr will die! And the dying will become data that will be fed into the Project. Then the Questioner will record the last few items and finish the work! The Project will be complete! The greatest act of sentience in the whole universe!"

"Insane," Thassyil said, shaking its head in a mixture of horror and wonder. "But what if the Questioner who answers your call won't do what you ask? What then?"

"But . . . but . . ." The Leader looked wildly at Thassyil. "It must! You must! We called you and you must help! You must do this last task so that the Project can be complete!"

Tell it, Thassyil, Seeker said silently. You know what's happening now. Tell the Leader.

I will, Thassyil replied, and thank you, Questioner. Thank you for everything.

Thassyil looked coldly at the Leader, its face a hard mask. "You're wrong, Leader. And the Project is wrong, too. The

Questioner you called doesn't have to help, won't help—indeed," Thassyil continued, its voice slightly mocking, "can't help."

"What?" the Leader shrieked. "What are you saying? Thassyil . . . Thassyil, is that you speaking? Tell the Questioner it must help! It must! The virus is ready to be distributed. The Project is prepared to enter its final stages. Tell the Questioner it must help!"

Thassyil smiled grimly and shrugged. "I'm afraid that's not possible, Leader."

"Not possible?! Not possible?! Why??!!"

"Because," Thassyil said calmly, drawing itself to its full height and turning away, "the Questioner is no longer here. It completed its mission and went back to its ship. I imagine that by now it is already on its way back to Labyrinth."

Epilogue

... and all at once I am nothing.
The soul is as mortal as the body.
But the knot of causes in which I am entangled
recurs and will create me again.
I myself belong to the causes of the eternal
  recurrence.

> Friedrich Nietzsche,
> Thus Spoke Zarathustra

※※※

"And that's the story," Seeker said, looking disconsolately down at the dusty ground of Start. "I guess I failed."

"Hmmmm, hmmmm," Longarm responded, looking thoughtfully off into the distance. "Failed, eh? That's what you think, eh?"

"Well, I certainly didn't answer any questions. Damn it, Teacher, the Vyinnlyirr are doomed just like their city is. Thassyil, Thryimm, Syssyir, the Leader, the whole lot don't have a hope. The city is disintegrating, falling into ruin, and all they can do is worry about their insane Project! There was nothing I could do to help them. So I left."

The Teacher cocked its head to one side and grinned broadly, a strange light glinting in its eyes. "You left, Novice, because your mission was complete. If there had been anything more to do, you can bet you'd still be there."

Seeker sighed deeply. "I suppose so. But I failed, Teacher."

Longarm just stared at Seeker, its face empty of emotion, a mask of seeming indifference. "Well, well, then you think you failed, eh? Did you at least learn anything?"

The Novice nodded slowly. "Yes. It's . . . it's hard to put in words . . . but Thassyil and I, well, we started out as enemies and ended up as friends." Seeker paused for a moment as a sorrowful expression crossed its face. "Damn. That's probably what I feel the worst about. Thassyil. I let Thassyil down. Abandoned it, just left when it was obvious there was nothing I could do."

"Just cut and ran, eh?"

"Basically, yes," Seeker replied gloomily.

"After what, almost a year of wandering around in the city, nearly dying in the waste, barely escaping death in the abyss, you just cut and ran. Couldn't stick it out to the end, eh?"

"But it really wasn't like that!" Seeker protested. "You don't understand! You weren't there. I . . ."

Longarm whooped a laugh, wrapped its arms around its chest and roared with peal after peal of hilarity. "Ah, ah, Seeker, you never change! That's what I like about you. You started a fool and you'll end up a fool! Ah, ah!"

The Teacher brought itself back under control with difficulty. Seeker stood there, embarrassed, not sure what to do or say. Finally the Teacher managed to gasp out, "Go away for a while. Take a walk out on Labyrinth. H*mb*l's out there somewhere."

"H*mb*l's still alive?" Seeker asked eagerly. "I'd wondered what had happened to the hummer but was almost afraid to ask. And Bilrog, have you heard from Bilrog?"

"Hmmmm. Yes. The Furmorian came back about, oh, several months ago. Bad shape. First mission a success in some ways, but Bilrog paid a heavy price. Very heavy. Patched it up best we could and sent it out again."

"Sent Bilrog back out? But why? If it was badly hurt shouldn't you have kept it here for a while?"

Longarm shrugged. "Dies here, dies there. What difference does it make? Except maybe if it dies there it might do somebody some good. Look, Seeker, go take a walk. Settle down, think about what happened to you. Let it trickle down into your mind. Look up H*mb*l, see how it's doing. Eh?"

Seeker mumbled agreement and wandered off.

It found the hummer about an hour out from Start. H*mb*l was dancing with a beast that was all fangs and claws. The two of them circled around each other in a weird rhythm of dips and sways, forwards and backs. Seeker just watched them for a while until the beast got tired of the dance and wandered off on some unknown errand. H*mb*l stood stock still as the creature left.

When it was gone, the hummer turned toward where Seeker was hiding and called out, "Seeker, come out, come out." Embarrassed, the Novice stood and waved at H*mb*l.

"Didn't know you saw me," it said as it walked up to its old friend. "Seemed to me you were concentrating on that thing."

"Yes, I was. But it was only a part of the total melody and counterpoint of the area. You introduced a new theme that I recognized from the past. You are back. You have completed your first mission."

Seeker unhappily looked at the ground. "Well, I guess 'completed' is a good neutral term for what happened." It paused, then suddenly blurted out, "I failed, H*mb*l. There was nothing I could do for them. And I abandoned a friend, Thassyil, my Vyinnlyirr host. I failed everyone."

H*mb*l buzzed softly and swayed sadly. "Failed? How can you say you failed?"

"Because I didn't save them!" Seeker cried out.

The hummer buzzed thoughtfully. "Success, saving, failure, losing. What do they mean in a case like this? What would it mean to save them, to succeed? To ruin the Project? To rebuild the city? What? And failure? To leave things as they were? To stop the Leader's plan to end the whole race? To give Thassyil something it never had before? Failure? Success? Those are narrow words, broad words, words that mean less than nothing while pretending to great significance."

Seeker stood staring at the hummer, its eyes wide and its mouth partly open in astonishment. "How . . . how do you know all that? Where did you hear . . ."

H*mb*l hummed a laugh. "You told Longarm, Longarm told Labyrinth, Labyrinth told me. It's all one big whole, Seeker, and you are part of it even if you don't know it."

"Part of it? I don't understand. I'm me and you're you and Labyrinth is a whole planet and . . ." Seeker's voice trailed off in wonder and confusion.

"All part of it," H*mb*l nodded, beginning to sway and move off. "All part of the same vast music. You, me, Bilrog, Darkhider, Thisunit, Longarm, Thassyil, all, all, part, part." And the hummer was gone.

* * *

The days passed slowly, almost languidly. Seeker wandered the surface of Labyrinth, totally at home among its many dangers. Now and then it saw H*mb*l in the distance. Twice it ran across the giant arachnid. On three occasions it moved the crystal. It had to kill several beasts that attacked it.

Finally the day came when Seeker went and found Longarm. "Teacher," it asked, "did I fail?"

Longarm hooted. "Did you? Why ask me? Ask yourself! But first tell me what it means to succeed!"

"I can't. But I still can't forget that I left Thassyil without any hope at all. Just left it."

"And what makes you so sure, first that you really left it behind, or second that you did nothing for it?" the Teacher asked gently.

Seeker looked startled. "But I did leave it. I went away back to the ship and . . ."

"Look into you own mind, Seeker. Look deeply into it and tell me what you find."

The Novice stared uncomprehendingly at the Teacher. Then it shrugged and turned its attention inward. There was a great deal of confusion on the surface, but that was quickly pushed aside. It was only a second until Seeker heard a trill of greeting. "Thassyil?" it asked in wonder.

"Who else?" the Vyinnlyirr replied. "I was beginning to think you'd forgotten me."

"But what . . . how did you get in here?"

Thassyil trilled a laugh. "You were in my mind and I was equally in yours. We are one now and always will be. Just as back in the city Thassyil carries you around with it, you carry me around with you."

"Then . . . then I didn't abandon Thassyil?"

"Oh, yes, you left. But you also stayed behind. Confusing, isn't it? And as for not doing anything for Thassyil, remember what I was like when we first met. Not the same Vyinnlyirr you left behind at all, eh?"

"No," Seeker said slowly, "no, rather different."

"And that is what you did for us in the city, Seeker," Thassyil said softly. "You gave us a new force: Thassyil."

"Just one Vyinnlyirr?"

"One very different Vyinnlyirr, Seeker. What more can any creature hope to accomplish? You changed one of us profoundly. And, I suspect, in the act changed our history just as profoundly."

"It isn't much..." Seeker said dubiously.

"It was a lot," Thassyil responded firmly. "Could you have made a major change, a complete revolution? Dismantled the Project? Brought the Vyinnlyirr of the city and the waste together? Repaired the machines? Not likely. The Leader, Thryimm, all the others would have fought that, especially coming from the outside. Thassyil, now, ah, foolish Thassyil, who knows what it can accomplish, working slowly, carefully, from within?"

Seeker was silent. It walked slowly away, leaving the Teacher behind without a word. Longarm's thick lips curved in a smile. "Seeker is learning," it muttered beneath its breath. Yes, came the reply in its mind. Yes.

"I am afraid of my own thoughts," Seeker said quietly to Longarm. "They circle around and around and come back to the same place."

"And what do you find at that place?" the Teacher asked gently.

"A great fear, a great horror, a great sickness. This circle is eternal, Longarm. This circle of fear and pain and life and death and struggle and searching for answers. It comes again and again. The past is always part of me, Thassyil is in me. Bilrog, Thisunit, Darkhider, H*mb*l, you, Labyrinth. It will go on and on as long as I exist."

"Long after you cease to exist, if it is possible to cease," Longarm said. "For all the others are like you and you are in them as they are in you. It is all one."

"It is all pain and anguish and defeat," Seeker wailed softly.

"Yes," Longarm answered. "And laughter and glory and victory. It recurs again and again and again. This day, these clouds, this pain, this fear, this wonder. Around and around, identical, endlessly."

"Then the worst will happen again! Nothing is ever saved."

"Yes! And nothing is ever lost! So embrace it, Seeker! Clutch it to you! Clutch the pain as well as the joy! It is all one!"

"But if all this is nothing, then I am nothing and all I have suffered is nothing! Everything is nothing!" Seeker's voice was harsh with bitterness.

"Precisely!" Longarm crowed exultantly. "And nothing is everything!"

"I can't stand it! It's too much to ask! It chokes me, fills me with fear! I can't stand it!" Seeker howled.

"It will be anyway!" Longarm roared back.

"The nausea!" Seeker raged.

"Yes!" the Teacher cried in ecstasy. "The nausea!"

Seeker's eyes were wide with wonder. "You know this?"

"I *am* this! And so are you! Open your arms to it, Seeker! Open to the eternity of pain and horror, pleasure and joy! Know it will come circling back endlessly! You are the cause and the caused. Know and embrace it! That will make you a Questioner! That and only that!"

Seeker stood and stared at the Teacher, its face twisted in anguish. "But . . . but then what is it all about? All the struggle, all the wandering through the waste, the abyss . . . Why?"

"Because it is! Throw your arms wide," Longarm commanded. "Only that way can you ever know! Open your arms and clutch the full emptiness to you!"

Seeker's expression was that of a creature torn by terror and desire and indecision. "I . . . I . . . there is so much to fear . . . so much that I . . ."

Then with a scream, it threw its arms wide. Its eyes bulged in its head and it shrieked again, the sound an incomprehensible mixture of ecstasy and horror, and collapsed.

Longarm stood looking down at the still body. "Now it begins," it said softly.

Yes, Labyrinth answered. Now it begins. Again.

THE FINEST THE UNIVERSE HAS TO OFFER

___THE OMEGA CAGE Steve Perry and Michael Reaves
0-441-62382-4/$3.50
The Omega Cage—a hi-tech prison for the special enemies of the brutal Confed. No one had ever escaped, but Dain Maro is about to attempt the impossible.

___THE WARLOCK'S COMPANION Christopher Stasheff
0-441-87341-3/$3.95
Fess, the beloved cyborg steed of Rod Gallowglass, has a host of revealing stories he's never shared. Now the Gallowglass children are about to hear the truth...from the horse's mouth.

___THE STAINLESS STEEL RAT Harry Harrison
0-441-77924-7/$3.50
The Stainless Steel Rat was the slickest criminal in the Universe until the police finally caught up with him. Then there was only one thing they could do—they made him a cop.

___DREAM PARK Larry Niven and Steven Barnes
0-441-16730-6/$4.95
Dream Park—the ultimate fantasy world where absolutely everything you ever dreamed of is real—including murder.

For Visa and MasterCard orders call: 1-800-631-8571

FOR MAIL ORDERS: CHECK BOOK(S). FILL OUT COUPON. SEND TO:

BERKLEY PUBLISHING GROUP
390 Murray Hill Pkwy., Dept. B
East Rutherford, NJ 07073

NAME_____

ADDRESS_____

CITY_____

STATE_____ ZIP_____

PLEASE ALLOW 6 WEEKS FOR DELIVERY.
PRICES ARE SUBJECT TO CHANGE WITHOUT NOTICE.

POSTAGE AND HANDLING:
$1.00 for one book, 25¢ for each additional. Do not exceed $3.50.

BOOK TOTAL	$ _____
POSTAGE & HANDLING	$ _____
APPLICABLE SALES TAX (CA, NJ, NY, PA)	$ _____
TOTAL AMOUNT DUE	$ _____

PAYABLE IN US FUNDS.
(No cash orders accepted.)

THE BEST OF NEW WAVE SCIENCE FICTION

__ Islands in the Net Bruce Sterling 0-441-37423-9/$4.50
Laura Webster is operating successfully in an age where information is power--until she's plunged into a netherworld of black-market pirates, new-age mercenaries, high-tech voodoo...and murder.

__ Neuromancer William Gibson 0-441-56959-5/$3.95
The novel of the year! Case was the best interface cowboy who ever ran in Earth's computer matrix. Then he double-crossed the wrong people...

__ Mirrorshades Bruce Sterling, editor
0-441-53382-5/$3.50
The definitive cyberpunk short fiction collection, including stories by William Gibson, Greg Bear, Pat Cadigan, Rudy Rucker, Lewis Shiner, and more.

__ Blood Music Greg Bear 0-441-06797-2/$3.50
Vergil Ulam had an idea to stop human entropy--"intelligent" cells--but they had a few ideas of their own.

__ Count Zero William Gibson 0-441-11773-2/$3.95
Enter a world where daring keyboard cowboys break into systems brain-first for mega-heists and brilliant aristocrats need an army of high-tech mercs to make a career move.

For Visa and MasterCard orders call: 1-800-631-8571

FOR MAIL ORDERS: CHECK BOOK(S). FILL OUT COUPON. SEND TO:

BERKLEY PUBLISHING GROUP
390 Murray Hill Pkwy., Dept. B
East Rutherford, NJ 07073

NAME_____
ADDRESS_____
CITY_____
STATE_____ ZIP_____

PLEASE ALLOW 6 WEEKS FOR DELIVERY.
PRICES ARE SUBJECT TO CHANGE WITHOUT NOTICE.

POSTAGE AND HANDLING:
$1.00 for one book, 25¢ for each additional. Do not exceed $3.50.

BOOK TOTAL $ ____
POSTAGE & HANDLING $ ____
APPLICABLE SALES TAX $ ____
(CA, NJ, NY, PA)
TOTAL AMOUNT DUE $ ____
PAYABLE IN US FUNDS.
(No cash orders accepted.)